1873

MISS OR MRS?
AND OTHER STORIES IN
OUTLINE

The novella is not bad,
though it has weaknesses.

The two short stories are
anecdotes without a twist.

WILKIE COLLINS

MISS OR MRS ?
AND OTHER STORIES IN OUTLINE

ALAN SUTTON PUBLISHING LIMITED

First published in 1872

First published in this edition in the United Kingdom in 1993
Alan Sutton Publishing Ltd
Phoenix Mill · Far Thrupp · Stroud · Gloucestershire · GL5 2BU

Copyright © in this edition
Alan Sutton Publishing Ltd 1993

Reprinted 1995

British Library Cataloguing in Publication Data

A catalogue record for this book is available from the British Library.

ISBN 0-7509-0454-2

Cover picture: detail from The Pink Gown *by John Waite Alexander (1856–1915), Whitford and Hughes,
London. (Photograph by Bridgeman Art Library, London)*

Typeset in 10/11 Bembo.
Typesetting and origination by
Alan Sutton Publishing Limited.
Printed in Great Britain by
The Guernsey Press Company Limited,
Guernsey, Channel Islands.

PREFACE

In their original form of publication, the stories contained in this volume were restricted within limits which alike precluded elaborate development of character and subtle handling of events. They are emphatically what I have called them on the title-page – Stories in Outline. As such, they take their modest place in the Gallery of Fiction. They have their attraction for the writer, as special studies in his Art; and their attention for the reader, as narratives which endeavour to interest him without making large demands on his attention and his time.

The first story in the present series originally appeared in the Christmas Number of the *Graphic* Illustrated Newspaper, for 1871. 'Miss or Mrs?' was fortunate enough to find its way at once to the favour of an unusually large circle of readers. In England and the English Colonies, in the United States, and on the Continent of Europe, I have to thank the public kindness, on this occasion, for the same hearty welcome.

The two shorter stories which follow were contributed to the Christmas Numbers of *All the Year Round*, for 1859 and 1861. Trifles as they are, they were both favourites with the kindest reader my works have ever had – my dear lost friend, Charles Dickens.

W.C.

London, December, 1872

CONTENTS

BIOGRAPHICAL NOTE

WILLIAM WILKIE COLLINS was born on 8 January 1824, in New Cavendish Street, London, the elder son of William Collins, a fashionable and successful painter of the early nineteenth century, who counted among his friends Wordsworth and Coleridge. William Collins was a religious man, and in his strict observances may have been a repressive influence on his son, who appears to have inherited his mother Harriet Geddes' attractive and friendly personality. Wilkie was named after his godfather, Sir David Wilkie, RA, a bachelor and close friend of the family.

Little is known of Wilkie's early life. His brother, Charles, was born in 1828, and the family lived comfortably, first in Hampstead, then in Bayswater, where Wilkie attended Maida Hill Academy. The following year the whole family left for Italy, where they spent two years, visiting the major art collections and learning Italian. On their return, Wilkie attended a private boarding school in Highbury, where his story-telling talent was recognized and exploited by a senior prefect who demanded, with the threat of physical violence, to be entertained. 'Thus', wrote Collins, 'I learnt to be amusing on a short notice and have derived benefit from those early lessons.'

When he left school in 1840, he showed no inclination to enter the Church, as his father wished, and chose, without enthusiasm, the world of commerce, accepting a post with Antrobus & Co., tea importers. He was totally unsuited to the regularity of business life, preferring to escape to the vibrant atmosphere of Paris. He started to write articles and short stories, which were accepted for publication, albeit anonymously, and in 1846 his father agreed that he should leave commerce and take up law, which would, in theory, provide him with a regular income. He studied at Lincoln's Inn Fields, and was finally called to the bar, but his legal knowledge was to be applied creatively in his novels, rather than practically in the law courts.

In his early twenties Collins painted as well as wrote. He had many friends who were artists, and he supported the new Pre-Raphaelite movement. In 1848 he had a picture exhibited in the Royal Academy. In the same year his first book was published: the memoirs of his father, who had died the previous year. These were diligently researched and provided a training ground for the emerging writer, developing his thorough methodical approach to compilation and exercising his descriptive ability. His first novel, *Antonia*, was published by Bentley's two years later. Although of no great literary merit, it was written in the then popular mode of historical romance, and so enjoyed instant success. The following year Bentley's published *Rambles beyond Railways*, an account of a holiday in Cornwall, which reflected Collins' life-long love of wild and remote places.

It was in the same year, 1851, that Wilkie Collins first met Charles Dickens, an introduction effected by their mutual friend, the artist, Augustus Egg. The meeting was significant for both, leading to a close friendship and working partnership from which both benefited. Dickens had found a friend of more stable temperament than himself, affable and tolerant, responsive to his restless demanding nature. From Collins he acquired the skill of economic and taut plotting, as evidenced in a *Tale of Two Cities* (which may be interestingly compared with Collins' story of the French Revolution, *Sister Rose*, 1855), and in his later novels. Collins was welcomed by the Dickens family, and spent many holidays with them in England and France. He was encouraged and guided in his writing by Dickens, and he must have been stimulated by the latter's enthusiasm and vitality. The two authors worked together on Dickens' magazines, *Household Words*, and *All the Year Round*. Collins was employed as an editor, and many of his works appeared first in these publications, while both writers collaborated on several short stories.

A Terribly Strange Bed – Collins' first work in the macabre genre – was the first of his short stories to appear in *Household Words*, in 1852. The following year the magazine saw the publication of *Gabriel's Marriage*, a story of a Breton fishing community. In the interim, Dickens had turned down *Mad Monkton*, a study of inherited insanity, as unsuitable subject matter, and this was later published by *Fraser's Magazine* in 1855. These, along with *Sister Rose, The Yellow Mask,* and *A Stolen Letter*, originally published in *Household Words*, were reprinted in *After Dark*, 1855, for which anthology Collins wrote the successfully economic and melodramatic *Lady of Glenwith Grange* (an inspiration for Miss Haversham?). *A Rogue's Life*, Collins' venture into the picaresque, was serialized in 1856. This was followed in 1857 by *The Dead Secret*, a full length novel, which in its complexity suggests the author's technical potential. *The Biter Bit*, which was published in 1858 and is commonly held to be the first humourous detective story, shows Collins' development of the epistolary form. Both of his two greatest novels, *A Woman in White* and *The Moonstone*, appeared first as serializations in *All the Year Round* – as did the less well known *No Name*. This unconventional study of illegitimacy was published in its full form in 1862, two years after the masterpiece of suspense and drama *A Woman in White* and six years before his original detective story, *The Moonstone*, appeared as complete books.

Another interest shared by Collins and Dickens was a love of the theatre. *The Frozen Deep*, 1857, written by Collins and starring Dickens, was inspired by an interest in the Arctic exploration of the time. It was followed by a series of minor productions, the stage version of *No Thoroughfare* (with combined authorship), enjoying a record run of two hundred nights in 1867.

Anyone meeting Collins in those days would have seen:

A neat figure of a cheerful plumpness, very small feet and hands, a full brown beard, a high and rounded forehead, a small nose not naturally intended to support a pair of large spectacles behind which his eyes shone with humour and friendship.

R.C. Lehmann, *Memories of Half a Century*

But how many would have glimpsed, as did the young artist, Rudolf Lehmann, the strange far-off look in his eyes, which gave the impression of investing 'almost everything with an air of mystery and romance'? It was suggestive of a depth of personality not accessible to many, but demonstrated by the author's expressed unconventional views of the class and social *mores* of the day; these were further borne out by what is known of his personal life. During the 1860s, Collins met and fell in love with Caroline Graves, who had a daughter by a previous marriage. He never married her, but lived with mother and daughter for most of the remainder of his life. In 1868, Caroline mysteriously married another, and Collins entered into a relationship with Martha Judd, by whom he had three children. However, by the early 1870s, he was once more living with Caroline, who was still known as Mrs Graves. It has been suggested that Martha Judd may have been employed originally by Collins as an amanuensis. Over the years Collins' health had been deteriorating. He was a victim of gout, which attacked his whole body, including his eyes. He suffered a particulary severe attack in 1868, when his mother died, and he was working on *The Moonstone*. A dedicated woman, capable of disregarding his suffering and attending only to his words was employed, to whom Collins dictated the rest of the work, but she has never been named.

In 1870 Charles Dickens died. During the previous ten years Collins had produced his best work: the three novels serialized in *All the Year Round; Armadale,* 1866, in the *Cornhill Magazine,* and *Man and Wife,* 1870, in *Cassell's Magazine*. But with Dickens' death, something in Collins seemed to die too, although his popularity remained undiminished. His novels, produced regularly until his death, were widely read, and his was some of the first fiction to appear in cheap editions. In the 1870s he enjoyed some success with the stage versions of his novels, which were produced both in London and the provinces. Two of Collins' novels were published in the early '70s; *Miss or Mrs?* in 1872, and *The New Magdalen* in 1873. Not only was Collins' work popular in England; his novels and plays were translated and produced in most European countries, including Russia, and were widely available in America. In

1873 Collins was invited to give readings in the eastern United States and Canada. Although his readings lacked the vitality of Dickens, the Americans were charmed by him.

Of course, it was not only Dickens' death which adversely affected Collins' work. His gout was becoming persistent, and he relied increasingly on laudanum to relieve the pain. However, he never lost his mental clarity, taking care to be properly informed about medicine, drugs and chemistry, as is clearly shown in *Heart and Science*, 1883 and the detailed notes he left for his last novel, *Blind Love*, 1890 – completed, posthumously, at his request, by Walter Besant. His novel *Legacy of Cain* was published in 1888, the year before he died. During his later years, his social life was restricted by poor health, but he did not become a recluse as has been suggested. He maintained close friendships with Charles Reade, Holman Hunt, the Beard and Lehmann families, and theatrical people, including Ada Cavendish and Mary Anderson. In 1889, after being involved in a cab accident, Collins' health rapidly declined, and he died while suffering from bronchitis on 23 September. He was buried at Kensal Green Cemetery.

SHEILA MICHELL

MISS OR MRS?

PERSONS OF THE STORY

Sir Joseph Graybrooke	(*Knight*)
Richard Turlington	(*Of the Levant Trade*)
Launcelot Linzie	(*Of the College of Surgeons*)
James Dicas	(*Of the Roll of Attorneys*)
Thomas Wildfang	(*Superannuated Seaman*)
Miss Graybrooke	(*Sir Joseph's Sister*)
Natalie	(*Sir Joseph's Daughter*)
Lady Winwood	(*Sir Joseph's Niece*)
Amelia Sophia } Dorothea	(*Lady Winwood's Stepdaughters*)

Period: The present time. *Place:* England.

FIRST SCENE

AT SEA

The night had come to an end. The new-born day waited for its quickening light in the silence that is never known on land – the silence before sunrise, in a calm at sea.

Not a breath came from the dead air. Not a ripple stirred on the motionless water. Nothing changed, but the softly-growing light; nothing moved but the lazy mist, curling up to meet the sun, its master, on the eastward sea. By fine gradations, the airy veil of morning thinned in substance as it rose – thinned, till there dawned through it in the first rays of sunlight the tall white sails of a Schooner Yacht.

From stem to stern silence possessed the vessel – as silence possessed the sea.

But one living creature was on deck – the man at the helm, dozing peaceably with his arm over the useless tiller. Minute by minute the light grew, and the heat grew with it; and still the helmsman slumbered, the heavy sails hung noiseless, the quiet water lay sleeping against the vessel's sides. The whole orb of the sun was visible above the water-line, when the first sound pierced its way through the morning silence. From far off over the shining white ocean, the cry of a sea-bird reached the yacht on a sudden out of the last airy circles of the waning mist.

The sleeper at the helm woke; looked up at the idle sails, and yawned in sympathy with them; looked out at the sea on either side of him, and shook his head obstinately at the superior obstinacy of the calm.

'Blow, my little breeze!' said the man, whistling the sailor's invocation to the wind softly between his teeth. 'Blow, my little breeze!'

'How's her head?' cried a bold and brassy voice, hailing the deck from the cabin staircase.

'Anywhere you like, master; all round the compass.'

The voice was followed by the man. The owner of the yacht appeared on deck.

Behold Richard Turlington, Esq., of the great Levant firm of Pizzituti, Turlington, and Branca! Aged eight-and-thirty; standing stiffly and sturdily at a height of not more than five feet six — Mr Turlington presented to the view of his fellow-creatures a face of the perpendicular order of human architecture. His forehead was a straight line, his upper lip was another, his chin was the straightest and the longest line of all. As he turned his swarthy countenance eastward, and shaded his light grey eyes from the sun, his knotty hand plainly revealed that it had got him his living by its own labour at one time or another in his life. Taken on the whole, this was a man whom it might be easy to respect, but whom it would be hard to love. Better company at the official desk than at the social table. Morally and physically — if the expression may be permitted — a man without a bend in him.

'A calm yesterday,' grumbled Richard Turlington, looking with stubborn deliberation all round him. 'And a calm to-day. Ha! next season I'll have the vessel fitted with engines. I hate this !'

'Think of the filthy coals, and the infernal vibration, and leave your beautiful schooner as she is. We are out for a holiday. Let the wind and the sea take a holiday too.'

Pronouncing those words of remonstrance, a slim, nimble, curly-headed young gentleman joined Richard Turlington on deck, with his clothes under his arm, his towels in his hand, and nothing on him but the nightgown in which he had stepped out of his bed.

'Launcelot Linzie, you have been received on board my vessel in the capacity of medical attendant on Miss Natalie Graybrooke, at her father's request. Keep your place, if you please. When I want your advice, I'll ask for it.' Answering in those terms, the elder man fixed his colourless grey eyes on the younger with an expression which added plainly: 'There won't be room enough in this schooner much longer for me and for you.'

Launcelot Linzie had his reasons (apparently) for declining to let his host offend him, on any terms whatever.

'Thank you!' he rejoined, in a tone of satirical good-humour. 'It isn't easy to keep my place on board your vessel. I can't help presuming to enjoy myself as if I was the owner. The life is such a new one – to *me*! It's so delightfully easy, for instance, to wash yourself here. On shore it's a complicated question of jugs and basins and tubs; one is always in danger of breaking something or spoiling something. Here you have only to jump out of bed, to run up on deck, and to do this!'

He turned, and scampered to the bows of the vessel. In one instant he was out of his nightgown, in another he was on the bulwark, in a third he was gambolling luxuriously in sixty fathoms of salt water.

Turlington's eyes followed him with a reluctant uneasy attention as he swam round the vessel, the only moving object in view. Turlington's mind, steady and slow in all its operations, set him a problem to be solved, on given conditions, as follows:–

'Launcelot Linzie is fifteen years younger than I am. Add to that, Launcelot Linzie is Natalie Graybrooke's cousin. Given those two advantages – Query: Has he taken Natalie's fancy?'

Turning that question slowly over and over in his mind, Richard Turlington seated himself in a corner at the stern of the vessel. He was still at work on the problem, when the young surgeon returned to his cabin to put the finishing touches to his toilet. He had not reached the solution when the steward appeared an hour later and said, 'Breakfast is ready, sir!'

They were a party of five round the cabin table.

First, Sir Joseph Graybrooke. Inheritor of a handsome fortune made by his father and his grandfather in trade. Mayor, twice elected, of a thriving provincial town. Officially privileged, while holding that dignity, to hand a silver trowel to a royal personage condescending to lay a first stone of a charitable edifice. Knighted accordingly, in honour of the occasion. Worthy of the honour and worthy of the occasion. A type of his eminently respectable class. Possessed of an amiable rosy face, and soft silky white hair. Sound in his principles; tidy in his dress; blest with moderate politics and a good digestion – a harmless, healthy, spruce, speckless, weak-minded old man.

Secondly, Miss Lavinia Graybrooke, Sir Joseph's maiden sister. Personally, Sir Joseph in petticoats. If you knew one you knew the other.

Thirdly, Miss Natalie Graybrooke – Sir Joseph's only child.

She had inherited the personal appearance and the temperament of her mother – dead many years since. There had been a mixture of Negro blood and French blood in the late Lady Graybrooke's family, settled originally in Martinique. Natalie had her mother's warm dusky colour, her mother's superb black hair, and her mother's melting lazy lovely brown eyes. At fifteen years of age (dating from her last birthday) she possessed the development of the bosom and limbs, which in England is rarely attained before twenty. Everything about the girl – except her little rosy ears – was on a grand Amazonian scale. Her shapely hand was long and large; her supple waist was the waist of a woman. The indolent grace of all her movements had its motive power in an almost masculine firmness of action, and profusion of physical resource. This remarkable bodily development was far from being accompanied by any corresponding development of character. Natalie's manner was the gentle, innocent manner of a young girl. She had her father's sweet temper engrafted on her mother's variable Southern nature. She moved like a goddess, and she laughed like a child. Signs of maturing too rapidly – of outgrowing her strength, as the phrase went – had made their appearance in Sir Joseph's daughter during the spring. The family doctor had suggested a sea-voyage, as a wise manner of employing the fine summer months. Richard Turlington's yacht was placed at her disposal – with Richard Turlington himself included as one of the fixtures of the vessel. With her father and her aunt to keep up round her the atmosphere of home – with cousin Launcelot (more commonly known as 'Launce') to carry out, if necessary, the medical treatment prescribed by superior authority on shore – the lovely invalid embarked on her summer cruise, and sprang

up into a new existence in the life-giving breezes of the sea.
After two happy months of lazy coasting round the shores of
England, all that remained of Natalie's illness was represented by
a delicious langour in her eyes, and an utter inability to devote
herself to anything which took the shape of a serious
occupation. As she sat at the cabin breakfast-table that morning,
in her quaintly-made sailing dress of old-fashioned nankeen –
her inbred childishness of manner contrasting delightfully with
the blooming maturity of her form – the man must have been
trebly armed indeed in the modern philosophy who could have
denied that the first of a woman's rights is the right of being
beautiful; and the foremost of a woman's merits, the merit of
being young!

The other two persons present at the table, were the two
gentlemen who have already appeared on the deck of the yacht.

'Not a breath of wind stirring!' said Richard Turlington. 'The
weather has got a grudge against us. We have drifted about four
or five miles in the last eight-and-forty hours. You will never
take another cruise with me – you must be longing to get on
shore.'

He addressed himself to Natalie: plainly eager to make
himself agreeable to the young lady – and plainly unsuccessful
in producing any impression on her. She made a civil answer;
and looked at her tea-cup, instead of looking at Richard
Turlington.

'You might fancy yourself on shore at this moment,' said
Launce. 'The vessel is as steady as a house, and the swing-table
we are eating our breakfast on is as even as your dining-room
table at home.'

He too addressed himself to Natalie – but without betraying
the anxiety to please her which had been shown by the other.
For all that, *he* diverted the girl's attention from her tea-cup;
and *his* idea instantly awakened a responsive idea in Natalie's
mind.

'It will be so strange on shore,' she said, 'to find myself in a
room that never turns on one side, and to sit at a table that
never tilts down to my knees at one time, or rises up to my
chin at another. How I shall miss the wash of the water at my

ear, and the ring of the bell on deck, when I am awake at night on land! No interest there in how the wind blows, or how the sails are set. No asking your way of the sun, when you are lost, with a little brass instrument and a morsel of pencil and paper. No delightful wandering wherever the wind takes you, without the worry of planning beforehand where you are to go. Oh, how I shall miss the dear changeable inconstant sea! And how sorry I am I'm not a man and a sailor!'

This to the guest, admitted on board on sufferance – and not one word of it addressed, even by chance, to the owner of the yacht!

Richard Turlington's heavy eyebrows contracted with an unmistakable expression of pain.

'If this calm weather holds,' he went on, addressing himself to Sir Joseph, 'I am afraid, Graybrooke, I shall not be able to bring you back to the port we sailed from, by the end of the week.'

'Whenever you like, Richard,' answered the old gentleman, resignedly. 'Any time will do for me.'

'Any time within reasonable limits, Joseph,' said Miss Lavinia – evidently feeling that her brother was conceding too much. She spoke with Sir Joseph's amiable smile and Sir Joseph's softly-pitched voice. Two twin babies could hardly have been more like one another.

While these few words were being exchanged among the elders, a private communication was in course of progress between the two young people, under the cabin table. Natalie's smartly-slippered foot felt its way cautiously inch by inch over the carpet till it touched Launce's boot. Launce, devouring his breakfast, instantly looked up from his plate – and then, at a second touch from Natalie, looked down again in a violent hurry. After pausing to make sure that she was not noticed, Natalie took up her knife. Under a perfectly-acted pretence of toying with it absently, in the character of a young lady absorbed in thought, she began dividing a morsel of ham left on the edge of her plate, into six tiny pieces. Launce's eye looked in sidelong expectation at the divided and subdivided ham. He was evidently waiting to see the collection of morsels put to some telegraphic use, previously determined on between his neighbour and himself.

In the mean while the talk proceeded among the other persons at the breakfast-table. Miss Lavinia addressed herself to Launce.

'Do you know, you careless boy, you gave me a fright this morning? I was sleeping with my cabin-window open, and I was awoke by an awful splash in the water. I called for the stewardess. I declare I thought somebody had fallen overboard!'

Sir Joseph looked up briskly; his sister had accidentally touched on an old association.

'Talking of falling overboard,' he began, 'reminds me of an extraordinary adventure——'

There Launce broke in, making his apologies.

'It shan't occur again, Miss Lavinia,' he said. 'To-morrow morning I'll oil myself all over, and slip into the water as silently as a seal.'

'Of an extraordinary adventure,' persisted Sir Joseph, 'which happened to me many years ago, when I was a young man. Lavinia?'

He stopped, and looked interrogatively at his sister. Miss Graybrooke nodded her head responsively, and settled herself in her chair, as if summoning her attention in anticipation of a coming demand on it. To persons well acquainted with the brother and sister these proceedings were ominous of an impending narrative, protracted to a formidable length. The two always told a story in couples, and always differed with each other about the facts, the sister politely contradicting the brother when it was Sir Joseph's story, and the brother politely contradicting the sister when it was Miss Lavinia's story. Separated one from the other, and thus relieved of their own habitual interchange of contradiction, neither of them had ever been known to attempt the relation of the simplest series of events, without breaking down.

'It was five years before I knew you, Richard,' proceeded Sir Joseph.

'Six years,' said Miss Graybrooke.

'Excuse me, Lavinia.'

'No, Joseph, I have it down in my diary.'

'Let us waive the point.' (Sir Joseph invariably used this formula as a means of at once conciliating his sister, and getting a fresh start for his story.) 'I was cruising off the Mersey in a Liverpool pilot-boat. I had hired the boat in company with a friend of mine, formerly notorious in London society, under the nickname (derived from the peculiar brown colour of his whiskers) of "Mahogany Dobbs."'

'The colour of his liveries, Joseph, not the colour of his whiskers.'

'My dear Lavinia, you are thinking of "Seagreen Shaw," so called from the extraordinary liveries he adopted for his servants in the year when he was sheriff.'

'I think not, Joseph.'

'I beg your pardon, Lavinia.'

Richard Turlington's knotty fingers drummed impatiently on the table. He looked towards Natalie. She was idly arranging her little morsels of ham in a pattern on her plate. Launcelot Linzie, still more idly, was looking at the pattern. Seeing what he saw now, Richard solved the problem which had puzzled him on deck. It was simply impossible that Natalie's fancy could be really taken by such an empty-headed fool as that!

Sir Joseph went on with his story –

'We were some ten or a dozen miles off the mouth of the Mersey——'

'Nautical miles, Joseph.'

'It doesn't matter, Lavinia.'

'Excuse me, brother, the late great and good Doctor Johnson said accuracy ought always to be studied even in the most trifling things.'

'They were common miles, Lavinia.'

'They were nautical miles, Joseph.'

'Let us waive the point. Mahogany Dobbs and I happened to be below in the cabin, occupied——'

Here Sir Joseph paused (with his amiable smile) to consult his memory. Miss Lavinia waited (with *her* amiable smile) for the coming opportunity of setting her brother right. At the same moment Natalie laid down her knife and softly touched Launce under the table. When she thus claimed his attention the six pieces of ham were arranged as follows in her plate:– Two pieces were placed opposite each other, and four pieces were ranged perpendicularly under them. Launce looked, and twice touched Natalie under the table. Interpreted by the Code agreed on between the two, the signal in the plate meant, 'I must see you in private.' And Launce's double touch anwered, 'After breakfast.'

Sir Joseph proceeded with his story. Natalie took up her knife again. Another signal coming!

'We were both down in the cabin, occupied in finishing our dinner——'

'Just sitting down to lunch, Joseph.'

'My dear! I ought to know.'

'I only repeat what I heard, brother. The last time you told the story, you and your friend were sitting down to lunch.'

'We won't particularize, Lavinia. Suppose we say occupied over a meal?'

'If it is of no more importance than that, Joseph, it would be surely better to leave it out altogether?'

'Let us waive the point. Well, we were suddenly alarmed by a shout on deck, "Man overboard!" We both rushed up the cabin stairs, naturally under the impression that one of our crew had fallen into the sea: an impression shared, I ought to add, by the man at the helm, who had given the alarm.'

Sir Joseph paused again. He was approaching one of the great dramatic points in his story, and was naturally anxious to present it as impressively as possible. He considered with himself, with his head a little on one side. Miss Lavinia considered with *herself*, with *her* head a little on one side. Natalie laid down her knife again, and again touched Launce under the table. This time there were five pieces of ham ranged longitudinally on the plate, with one piece immediately under them at the centre of the line. Interpreted by the Code, this signal indicated two ominous words, 'Bad news.' Launce looked significantly at the owner of the yacht (meaning of the look, 'Is he at the bottom of it?'). Natalie frowned in reply (meaning of the frown, 'Yes, he is'). Launce looked down again into the plate. Natalie instantly pushed all the pieces of ham together in a little heap (meaning of the heap, 'No more to say').

'Well?' said Richard Turlington, turning sharply on Sir Joseph. 'Get on with your story. What next?'

Thus far he had not troubled himself to show even a decent pretence of interest in his old friend's perpetually-interrupted narrative. It was only when Sir Joseph had reached his last sentence – intimating that the man overboard might turn out in course of time not to be a man of the pilot-boat's crew – it was only then that Turlington sat up in his chair, and showed signs of suddenly feeling a strong interest in the progress of the story.

Sir Joseph went on –

'As soon as we got on deck, we saw the man in the water, astern. Our vessel was hove up in the wind, and the boat was lowered. The master and one of the men took the oars. All told, our crew were seven in number. Two away in the boat, a third at the helm, and, to my amazement, when I looked round, the other four behind me, making our number complete. At the same moment Mahogany Dobbs, who was looking through a telescope, called out, "Who the devil can he be? The man is floating on a hen-coop, and we have got nothing of the sort on board this pilot-boat."'

The one person present who happened to notice Richard Turlington's face when those words were pronounced was Launcelot Linzie. He – and he alone – saw the Levant trader's swarthy complexion fade slowly to a livid ashen grey; his eyes the while fixing themselves on Sir Joseph Graybrooke with a furtive glare in them like the glare in the eyes of a wild beast. Apparently conscious that Launce was looking at him – though he never turned his head Launce's way – he laid his elbow on the table, lifted his arm, and so rested his face on his hand, while the story went on, as to screen it effectually from the young surgeon's view.

'The man was brought on board,' proceeded Sir Joseph, 'sure enough with a hen-coop – on which he had been found floating. The poor wretch was blue with terror and exposure in the water; he fainted when we lifted him on deck. When he came to himself he told us a horrible story. He was a sick and destitute foreign seaman, and he had hidden himself in the hold of an English vessel (bound to a port in his native country) which had sailed from Liverpool that morning. He had been discovered, and brought before the captain. The captain, a monster in human form, if ever there was one yet——'

Before the next word of the sentence could pass Sir Joseph's lips, Turlington startled the little party in the cabin by springing suddenly to his feet.

'The breeze!' he cried; 'the breeze at last!'

As he spoke, he wheeled round to the cabin door so as to turn his back on his guests, and hailed the deck.

'Which way is the wind?'

'There is not a breath of wind, sir.'

Not the slightest movement in the vessel had been perceptible in the cabin; not a sound had been audible indicating the rising of the breeze. The owner of the yacht – accustomed to the sea; capable, if necessary, of sailing his own vessel – had surely committed a strange mistake! He turned again to his friends, and made his apologies with an excess of polite regret, far from characteristic of him at other times, and under other circumstances.

'Go on,' he said to Sir Joseph, when he had got to the end of his excuses; 'I never heard such an interesting story in my life. Pray go on!'

The request was not an easy one to comply with. Sir Joseph's ideas had been thrown into confusion. Miss Lavinia's contradictions (held in reserve) had been scattered beyond recall. Both brother and sister were, moreover, additionally hindered in recovering the control of their own resources by the look and manner of their host. He alarmed, instead of encouraging the two harmless old people, by fronting them almost fiercely, with his elbows squared on the table, and his face expressive of a dogged resolution to sit there and listen, if need be, for the rest of his life. Launce was the person who set Sir Joseph going again. After first looking attentively at Richard, he took his uncle straight back to the story by means of a question thus:—

'You don't mean to say that the captain of the ship threw the man overboard?'

'That is just what he did, Launce. The poor wretch was too
ill to work his passage. The captain declared he would have no
idle foreign vagabond in his ship to eat up the provisions of
Englishmen who worked. With his own hands he cast the hen-
coop into the water, and (assisted by one of his sailors) he threw
the man after it, and told him to float back to Liverpool with
the evening tide.'

'A lie!' cried Turlington, addressing himself, not to Sir
Joseph, but to Launce.

'Are you acquainted with the circumstances?' asked Launce,
quietly.

'I know nothing about the circumstances. I say, from my
own experience, that foreign sailors are even greater
blackguards than English sailors. The man had met with an
accident, no doubt. The rest of his story was a lie – and the
object of it was to open Sir Joseph's purse.'

Sir Joseph mildly shook his head.

'No lie, Richard. Witnesses proved that the man had spoken
the truth.'

'Witnesses? Pooh! More liars, you mean.'

'I went to the owners of the vessel,' pursued Sir Joseph. 'I got
from them the names of the officers and the crew; and I waited,
leaving the case in the hands of the Liverpool police. The ship
was wrecked at the mouth of the Amazon. But the crew and the
cargo were saved. The men belonging to Liverpool came back.
They were a bad set, I grant you. But they were examined
separately about the treatment of the foreign sailor, and they all
told the same story. They could give no account of their captain,
nor of the sailor who had been his accomplice in the crime,
except that they had not embarked in the ship which brought the
rest of the crew to England. Whatever may have become of the
captain since, he certainly never returned to Liverpool.'

'Did you find out his name?'

The question was asked by Turlington. Even Sir Joseph, the
least observant of men, noticed that it was put with a perfectly
unaccountable irritability of manner.

'Don't be angry, Richard,' said the old gentleman. 'What is
there to be angry about?'

'I don't know what you mean. I'm not angry – I'm only curious. *Did* you find out who he was?'

'I did. His name was Goward. He was well-known at Liverpool as a very clever and a very dangerous man. Quite young at the time I am speaking of, and a first-rate sailor: famous for taking command of unseaworthy ships and vagabond crews. Report described him to me as having made considerable sums of money in that way, for a man in his position; serving firms, you know, with a bad name, and running all sorts of desperate risks. A sad ruffian, Richard! More than once in trouble, on both sides of the Atlantic, for acts of violence and cruelty. Dead, I daresay, long since.'

'Or possibly,' said Launce, 'alive, under another name, and thriving in a new way of life, with more desperate risks in it, of some other sort.'

'Are *you* acquainted with the circumstances?' asked Turlington, retorting Launce's question on him, with a harsh ring of defiance in his brassy voice.

'What became of the poor foreign sailor, papa?' said Natalie; purposely interrupting Launce before he could meet the question angrily asked of him, by an angry reply.

'We made a subscription, and spoke to his consul, my dear. He went back to his country, poor fellow, comfortably enough.'

'And there is an end of Sir Joseph's story,' said Turlington, rising noisily from his chair. 'It's a pity we haven't got a literary man on board – he would make a novel of it.' He looked up at the skylight as he got on his feet. 'Here is the breeze, this time,' he exclaimed, 'and no mistake!'

It was true. At last the breeze had come. The sails flapped, the main boom swung over with a thump, and the stagnant water, stirred at last, bubbled merrily past the vessel's sides.

'Come on deck, Natalie, and get some fresh air,' said Miss Lavinia, leading the way to the cabin-door.

Natalie held up the skirt of her nankeen dress, and exhibited the purple trimming torn away over an extent of some yards.

'Give me half an hour first, aunt, in my cabin,' she said, 'to mend this.'

Miss Lavinia elevated her venerable eyebrows in amazement.

'You have done nothing but tear your dresses, my dear, since you have been in Mr Turlington's yacht. Most extraordinary! I have torn none of mine during the whole cruise.'

Natalie's dark colour deepened a shade. She laughed a little uneasily. 'I am so awkward on board ship,' she replied, and turned away, and shut herself up in her cabin.

Richard Turlington produced his case of cigars.

'Now is the time,' he said to Sir Joseph 'for the best cigar of the day – the cigar after breakfast. Come on deck.'

'You will join us, Launce?' said Sir Joseph.

'Give me half an hour first, over my books,' Launce replied. 'I mustn't let my medical knowledge get musty at sea, and I might not feel inclined to study later in the day.'

'Quite right, my dear boy, quite right.'

Sir Joseph patted his nephew approvingly on the shoulder. Launce turned away on *his* side, and shut himself up in his cabin.

The other three ascended together to the deck.

SECOND SCENE

THE STORE-ROOM

Persons possessed of sluggish livers and tender hearts find two serious drawbacks to the enjoyment of a cruise at sea. It is exceedingly difficult to get enough walking exercise; and it is next to impossible (where secrecy is an object) to make love without being found out. Reverting for the moment to the latter difficulty only, life within the narrow and populous limits of a vessel may be defined as essentially life in public. From morning to night you are in your neighbour's way, or your neighbour is in your way. As a necessary result of these conditions, the rarest of existing men may be defined as the man who is capable of stealing a kiss at sea without discovery. An inbred capacity for stratagem of the finest sort; inexhaustible inventive resources; patience which can flourish under superhuman trials; presence of mind which can keep its balance victoriously under every possible stress of emergency – these are some of the qualifications which must accompany Love on a cruise, when Love embarks in the character of a contraband commodity not duly entered on the papers of the ship.

Having established a Code of Signals which enabled them to communicate privately, while the eyes and ears of others were wide open on every side of them, Natalie and Launce were next confronted by the more serious difficulty of finding a means of meeting together at stolen interviews on board the yacht. Possessing none of those precious moral qualifications already enumerated as the qualifications of an accomplished lover at sea, Launce had proved unequal to grapple with the obstacles in his way. Left to her own inventive resources, Natalie had first suggested the young surgeon's medical studies as Launce's unanswerable excuse for shutting himself up at intervals in the lower regions – and had then hit on the happy idea of tearing her trimmings, and condemning herself to repair her own carelessness, as the all-sufficient reason for similar acts of self-seclusion on her side. In this way the lovers contrived, while the innocent ruling authorities were on deck, to meet privately below them, on the neutral ground of the main cabin – and there, by previous arrangement at the breakfast-table, they were about to meet privately now.

Natalie's door was, as usual on these occasions, the first that opened; for this sound reason, that Natalie's quickness was the quickness to be depended on in case of accident.

She looked up at the skylight. There were the legs of the two gentlemen and the skirts of her aunt visible (and stationary) on the lee side of the deck. She advanced a few steps and listened. There was a pause in the murmur of the voices above. She looked up again. One pair of legs (not her father's) had disappeared. Without an instant's hesitation, Natalie darted back to her own door, just in time to escape Richard Turlington descending the cabin stairs. All he did was to go to one of the drawers under the main-cabin book-case, and to take out a map, ascending again immediately to the deck. Natalie's guilty conscience rushed instantly, nevertheless, to the conclusion that Richard suspected her. When she showed herself for the second time, instead of venturing into the cabin, she called across it in a whisper,

'Launce!'

Launce appeared at his door. He was peremptorily checked before he could cross the threshold.

'Don't stir a step! Richard has been down in the cabin! Richard suspects us!'

'Nonsense! Come out.'

'Nothing will induce me, unless you can find some other place than the cabin.'

Some other place? How easy to find it on land! How apparently impossible at sea! There was the forecastle (full of men) at one end of the vessel. There was the sail-room (full of sails) at the other. There was the ladies' cabin (used as the ladies' dressing-room; inaccessible, in that capacity, to every male human being on board). Was there any disposable enclosed space to be found amidships? On one side there were the sleeping-berths of the sailing master and his mate (impossible to borrow *them*). On the other side was the steward's store-room. Launce considered for a moment. The steward's store-room was just the thing!

'Where are you going?' asked Natalie, as her lover made straight for a closed door at the lower extremity of the main-cabin.

'To speak to the steward, darling. Wait one moment, and you will see me again.'

Launce opened the store-room door, and discovered, not the steward, but his wife, who occupied the situation of stewardess on board the vessel. The accident was, in this case, a lucky one. Having stolen several kisses at sea, and having been discovered (in every case) either by the steward or his wife, Launce felt no difficulty in prefacing his request to be allowed the use of the room by the plainest allusion to his relations with Natalie. He could count on the silence of the sympathizing authorities in this region of the vessel, having wisely secured them as accomplices by the usual persuasion of the pecuniary sort. Of the two, however, the stewardess, as a woman, was the more likely to lend a ready ear to Launce's entreaties in his present emergency. After a faint show of resistance, she consented, not only to leave the room, but to keep her husband out of it, on the understanding that it was not to be occupied for more than ten minutes. Launce made the signal to Natalie at one door, while the stewardess went out by the other. In a moment more the lovers were united in a private room. Is it necessary to say in what language the proceedings were opened? Surely not! There is an inarticulate language of the lips in use on these occasions in which we are all proficient, though we sometimes forget it in later life. Natalie seated herself on a locker. The tea, sugar, and spices were at her back, a side of bacon swung over her head, and a net full of lemons dangled before her face. It might not be roomy, but it was snug and comfortable.

'Suppose they call for the steward?' she suggested. ('Don't, Launce!')

'Never mind. We shall be safe enough if they do. The steward has only to show himself on deck, and they will suspect nothing.'

'Do be quiet, Launce! I have got dreadful news to tell you. And, besides, my aunt will expect to see me with my braid sewn on again.'

She had brought her needle and thread with her. Whipping up the skirt of her dress on her knee, she bent forward over it, and set herself industriously to the repair of the torn trimming. In this position her lithe figure showed charmingly its firm yet easy line. The needle, in her dexterous brown fingers, flew through its work. The locker was a broad one; Launce was able to seat himself partially behind her. In this position who could have resisted the temptation to lift up her great knot of broadly-plaited black hair, and to let the warm, dusky nape of her neck disclose itself to view? Who, looking at it, could fail to revile the senseless modern fashion of dressing the hair, which hides the double beauty of form and colour that nestles at the back of a woman's neck? From time to time, as the interview proceeded, Launce's lips emphasized the more important words occurring in his share of the conversation on the soft fragrant skin which the lifted hair let him see at intervals. In Launce's place, sir, you would have done it too.

'Now, Natalie, what is the news?'

'He has spoken to papa, Launce.'

'Richard Turlington?'

'Yes.'

'Damn him!'

Natalie started. A curse addressed to the back of your neck, instantly followed by a blessing in the shape of a kiss, *is* a little trying when you are not prepared for it.

'Don't do that again, Launce! It was while you were on deck, smoking, and when I was supposed to be fast asleep. I opened the ventilator in my cabin door, dear, and I heard every word they said. He waited till my aunt was out of the way, and he had got papa all to himself, and then he began it in that horrible, downright voice of his – "Graybrooke! how much longer am I to wait?" '

'Did he say that?'

'No more swearing, Launce! Those were the words. Papa didn't understand them. He only said (poor dear!) – "Bless my soul, Richard, what do you want?" Richard soon explained himself. "Who could he be waiting for – but Me?" Papa said something about my being so young. Richard stopped his mouth directly. "Girls were like fruit; some ripened soon, and some ripened late. Some were women at twenty, and some were women at sixteen. It was impossible to look at me, and not see that I was like a new being after my two months at sea," and so on and so on. Papa behaved like an angel. He still tried to put it off. "Plenty of time, Richard, plenty of time." "Plenty of time for *her*" (was the wretch's answer to that); "but not for *me*. Think of all I have to offer her" (as if I cared for his money!); "think how long I have looked upon her as growing up to be my wife" (growing up for *him* – monstrous!), "and don't keep me in a state of uncertainty, which it gets harder and harder for a man in my position to endure!" He was really quite eloquent. His voice trembled. There is no doubt, dear, that he is very, very fond of me.'

'And you feel flattered by it, of course?'

'Don't talk nonsense. I feel a little frightened at it, I can tell you.'

'Frightened? Did *you* notice him this morning?'

'I? When?'

'When your father was telling that story about the man overboard.'

'No. What did he do? Tell me, Launce.'

'I'll tell you directly. How did it all end last night? Did your father make any sort of promise?'

'You know Richard's way; Richard left him no other choice. Papa had to promise before he was allowed to go to bed.'

'To let Turlington marry you?'

'Yes; the week after my next birthday.'

'The week after next Christmas Day?'

'Yes. Papa is to speak to me as soon as we are at home again, and my married life is to begin with the New Year.'

'Are you in earnest, Natalie? Do you really mean to say it has gone as far as that?'

'They have settled everything. The splendid establishment we are to set up, the great income we are to have. I heard papa tell Richard that half his fortune should go to me on my wedding-day. It was sickening to hear how much they made of Money, and how little they thought of Love. What am I to do, Launce?'

'That's easily answered, my darling. In the first place, you are to make up your mind not to marry Richard Turlington——'

'Do talk reasonably. You know I have done all I could. I have told papa that I can think of Richard as a friend, but not as a husband. He only laughs at me, and says, "Wait a little, and you will alter your opinion, my dear." You see Richard is everything to him; Richard has always managed his affairs, and has saved him from losing by bad speculations; Richard has known me from the time when I was a child; Richard has a splendid business, and quantities of money. Papa can't even imagine that I can resist Richard. I have tried my aunt; I have told her he is too old for me. All she says is, "Look at your father; he was much older than your mother, and what a happy marriage theirs was." Even if I said in so many words, "I won't

marry Richard," what good would it do to *us*? Papa is the best
and dearest old man in the world; but oh, he is so fond of
money! He believes in nothing else. He would be furious – yes,
kind as he is, he would be furious – if I even hinted that I was
fond of *you*. Any man who proposed to marry me – if he
couldn't match the fortune that I should bring him by a fortune
of his own – would be a lunatic in papa's eyes. He wouldn't
think it necessary to answer him; he would ring the bell, and
have him shown out of the house. I am exaggerating nothing,
Launce; you know I am speaking the truth. There is no hope in
the future – that I can see – for either of us.'

'Have you done, Natalie? I have something to say on my side
if you have.'

'What is it?'

'If things go on as they are going on now, shall I tell you how
it will end? It will end in your being Turlington's wife.'

'Never!'

'So you say now; but you don't know what may happen
between this and Christmas Day. Natalie, there is only one way
of making sure that you will never marry Richard. Marry *me*.'

'Without papa's consent?'

'Without saying a word to anybody till it's done.'

'Oh, Launce! Launce!'

'My darling, every word you have said proves there is no
other way. Think of it, Natalie, think of it.'

There was a pause. Natalie dropped her needle and thread,
and hid her face in her hands. 'If my poor mother was only
alive,' she said; 'if I only had an elder sister to advise me, and to
take my part.'

She was evidently hesitating. Launce took a man's advantage
of her indecision. He pressed her without mercy.

'Do you love me?' he whispered, with his lips close to her
ear.

'You know I do, dearly.'

'Put it out of Richard's power to part us, Natalie.'

'Part us? We are cousins: we have known each other since
we were both children. Even if he proposed parting us, papa
wouldn't allow it.'

'Mark my words, he *will* propose it. As for your father, Richard has only to lift his finger and your father obeys him. My love, the happiness of both our lives is at stake.' He wound his arm round her, and gently drew her head back on his bosom. 'Other girls have done it, darling,' he pleaded, 'why shouldn't you?'

The effort to answer him was too much for her. She gave it up. A low sigh fluttered through her lips. She nestled closer to him, and faintly closed her eyes. The next instant she started up, trembling from head to foot, and looked at the skylight. Richard Turlington's voice was suddenly audible on deck exactly above them.

'Graybrooke, I want to say a word to you about Launcelot Linzie.'

Natalie's first impulse was to fly to the door. Hearing Launce's name on Richard's lips, she checked herself. Something in Richard's tone roused in her the curiosity which suspends fear. She waited, with her hand in Launce's hand.

'If you remember,' the brassy voice went on, 'I doubted the wisdom of taking him with us on this cruise. You didn't agree with me, and, at your express request, I gave way. I did wrong. Launcelot Linzie is a very presuming young man.'

Sir Joseph's answer was accompanied by Sir Joseph's mellow laugh.

'My dear Richard! Surely you are a little hard on Launce?'

'You are not an observant man, Graybrooke. I am. I see signs of his presuming with all of us, and especially with Natalie. I don't like the manner in which he speaks to her, and looks at her. He is unduly familiar; he is insolently confidential. There must be a stop put to it. In my position, my feelings ought to be regarded. I request you to check the intimacy when we get on shore.'

Sir Joseph's next words were spoken more seriously. He expressed his surprise.

'My dear Richard, they are cousins, they have been playmates from childhood. How *can* you think of attaching the slightest importance to anything that is said or done by poor Launce?'

There was a good-humoured contempt in Sir Joseph's reference to 'poor Launce' which jarred on his daughter. He might almost have been alluding to some harmless domestic animal. Natalie's colour deepened. Her hand pressed Launce's hand gently.

Turlington still persisted.

'I must once more request – seriously request – that you will check this growing intimacy. I don't object to your asking him to the house when you ask other friends. I only wish you (and expect you) to stop his "dropping in," as it is called, at any hour of the day or evening when he may have nothing to do. Is that understood between us?'

'If you make a point of it, Richard, of course it's understood between us.'

Launce looked at Natalie, as weak Sir Joseph consented in those words.

'What did I tell you?' he whispered.

Natalie hung her head in silence. There was a pause in the conversation on deck. The two gentlemen walked away slowly towards the forward part of the vessel.

Launce pursued his advantage.

'Your father leaves us no alternative,' he said. 'The door will be closed against me as soon as we get on shore. If I lose you, Natalie, I don't care what becomes of me. My profession may go to the devil. I have nothing left worth living for.'

'Hush! hush! don't talk in that way!'

Launce tried the soothing influence of persuasion once more.

'Hundreds and hundreds of people in our situation have married privately – and have been forgiven afterwards,' he went on. 'I won't ask you to do anything in a hurry. I will be guided entirely by your wishes. All I want to quiet my mind is to know that you are mine. Do, do, do make me feel sure that Richard Turlington can't take you away from me.'

'Don't press me, Launce.' She dropped on the locker. 'See!' she said. 'It makes me tremble only to think of it!'

'Who are you afraid of, darling? Not your father, surely?'

'Poor papa! I wonder whether he would be hard on me for the first time in his life?' She stopped; her moistening eyes looked up imploringly in Launce's face. 'Don't press me!' she repeated faintly. 'You know it's wrong. We should have to confess it – and then what would happen?' She paused again. Her eyes wandered nervously to the deck. Her voice dropped to its lowest tones. 'Think of Richard!' she said, and shuddered at the terrors which that name conjured up. Before it was possible to say a quieting word to her, she was again on her feet. Richard's name had suddenly recalled to her memory Launce's mysterious allusion, at the outset of the interview, to the owner of the yacht. 'What was that you said about Richard just now?' she asked. 'You saw something (or heard something) strange while papa was telling his story. What was it?'

'I noticed Richard's face, Natalie, when your father told us that the man overboard was not one of the pilot-boat's crew. He turned ghastly pale. He looked guilty——'

'Guilty? Of what?'

'He was present – I am certain of it – when the sailor was thrown into the sea. For all I know, he may have been the man who did it.'

Natalie started back in horror.

'Oh, Launce! Launce! that is too bad. You may not like Richard – you may treat Richard as your enemy. But to say such a horrible thing of him as that – ! It's not generous. It's not like *you*.'

'If you had seen him you would have said it too. I mean to make inquiries – in your father's interests as well as in ours. My brother knows one of the Commissioners of Police; and my brother can get it done for me. Turlington has not always been in the Levant trade – I know that already.'

'For shame, Launce! for shame!'

The footsteps on deck were audible, coming back. Natalie sprang to the door leading into the cabin. Launce stopped her, as she laid her hand on the lock. The footsteps went straight on towards the stern of the vessel. Launce clasped both arms round her. Natalie gave way.

'Don't drive me to despair!' he said. 'This is my last opportunity. I don't ask you to say at once that you will marry me – I only ask you to think of it. My darling! my angel! will you think of it?'

As he put the question, they might have heard (if they had not been too completely engrossed in each other to listen) the footsteps returning – one pair of footsteps only, this time. Natalie's prolonged absence had begun to surprise her aunt, and had roused a certain vague distrust in Richard's mind. He walked back again along the deck by himself. He looked absently into the main-cabin as he passed it. The store-room skylight came next. In his present frame of mind would he look absently into the store-room too?

'Let me go!' said Natalie.

Launce only answered, 'Say yes,' and held her as if he would never let her go again.

At the same moment Miss Lavinia's voice rose shrill from the deck, calling for Natalie. There was but one way of getting free from him. She said, 'I'll think of it.' Upon that, he kissed her and let her go.

The door had barely closed on her when the lowering face of Richard Turlington appeared on a level with the side of the skylight – looking down into the store-room at Launce.

'Hullo!' he called out roughly. 'What are you doing in the steward's room?'

Launce took up a box of matches on the dresser. 'I'm getting a light,' he answered readily.

'I allow nobody below, forward of the main-cabin, without my leave. The steward has permitted a breach of discipline on board my vessel. The steward will leave my service.'

'The steward is not to blame.'

'I am the judge of that. Not you.'

Launce opened his lips to reply. An outbreak between the two men appeared to be inevitable – when the sailing-master of the yacht joined his employer on deck, and directed Turlington's attention to a question which is never to be trifled with at sea, the question of wind and tide.

The yacht was then in the Bristol Channel, at the entrance to Bideford Bay. The breeze, fast freshening, was also fast changing the direction from which it blew. The favourable tide had barely three hours more to run.

'The wind's shifting, sir,' said the sailing-master. 'I'm afraid we shan't get round the point this tide, unless we lay her off on the other tack.'

Turlington shook his head.

'There are letters waiting for me at Bideford,' he said. 'We have lost two days in the calm. I must send ashore to the Post-office, whether we lose the tide or not.'

The vessel held on her course. Off the port of Bideford, the boat was sent ashore to the Post-office; the yacht standing off and on, waiting the appearance of the letters. In the shortest time in which it was possible to bring them on board, the letters were in Turlington's hands.

The men were hauling the boat up to the davits, the yacht was already heading off from the land, when Turlington startled everybody by one peremptory word – 'Stop!'

He had thrust all his letters but one into the pocket of his sailing jacket, without reading them. The one letter which he had opened, he held in his closed hand. Rage was in his staring eyes; consternation was on his pale lips.

'Lower the boat!' he shouted; 'I must get to London to-night.' He stopped Sir Joseph, approaching him with open mouth. 'There's no time for questions and answers. I must get back.' He swung himself over the side of the yacht, and addressed the sailing-master from the boat. 'Save the tide if you can; if you can't, put them ashore to-morrow, at Minehead, or Watchet – wherever they like.' He beckoned to Sir Joseph to lean over the bulwark, and hear something he had to say in private. 'Remember what I told you about Launcelot Linzie!' he whispered fiercely. His parting look was for Natalie. He spoke to her with a strong constraint on himself, as gently as he could. 'Don't be alarmed; I shall see you in London.' He seated himself in the boat, and took the tiller. The last words they heard him say were words urging the men at the oars to lose no time. He was invariably brutal with the men. 'Pull, you lazy beggars!' he exclaimed, with an oath. 'Pull for your lives!'

THIRD SCENE

THE MONEY MARKET

Let us be serious. – Business!

The new scene plunges us head-foremost into the affairs of the Levant trading-house of Pizzituti, Turlington, and Branca. What on earth do we know about the Levant Trade? Courage! If we have ever known what it is to want money, we are perfectly familiar with the subject at starting. The Levant Trade does occasionally get into difficulties. – Turlington wanted money.

The letter which had been handed to him on board the yacht was from his third partner, Mr Branca, and was thus expressed:–

'A crisis in the trade. All right, so far – except our business with the small foreign firms. Bills to meet from those quarters (say), forty thousand pounds – and, I fear, no remittances to cover them. Paticulars stated in another letter addressed to you at Post-office, Ilfracombe. I am quite broken down with anxiety, and confined to my bed. Pizzituti is still detained at Smyrna. Come back at once.'

The same evening Turlington was at his office in Austin Friars, investigating the state of affairs, with his head clerk to help him.

Stated briefly, the business of the firm was of the widely miscellaneous sort. They plied a brisk trade, in a vast variety of commodities. Nothing came amiss to them, from Manchester cotton manufactures to Smyrna figs. They had branch houses at Alexandria and Odessa; and correspondents, here, there, and everywhere, along the shores of the Mediterranean, and in the ports of the East. These correspondents were the persons alluded to in Mr Branca's letter, as 'small foreign firms'; and they had produced the serious financial crisis in the affairs of the great house in Austin Friars, which had hurried Turlington up to London.

Every one of these minor firms claimed, and received, the privilege of drawing bills on Pizzituti, Turlington, and Branca, for amounts varying from four to six thousand pounds – on no better security than a verbal understanding that the money to pay the bills should be forwarded before they fell due. Competition, it is needless to say, was at the bottom of this insanely reckless system of trading. The native firms laid it down as a rule, that they would decline to transact business with any house in the trade which refused to grant them their privilege. In the case of Turlington's house, the foreign merchants had drawn their bills on him for sums, large in the aggregate, if not large in themselves; had, long since, turned those bills into cash in their own markets, for their own necessities; and had now left the money which their paper represented, to be paid by their London correspondents as it fell due. In some instances, they had sent nothing but promises and excuses. In others, they had forwarded drafts on firms which had failed already, or which were about to fail, in the crisis. After first exhausting his resources in ready money, Mr Branca had provided for the more pressing necessities, by pledging the credit of the house, so far as he *could* pledge it without exciting suspicion of the truth. This done, there were actually left, between that time and Christmas, liabilities to be met to the extent of forty thousand pounds, without a farthing in hand to pay that formidable debt.

After working through the night, this was the conclusion at which Richard Turlington arrived, when the rising sun looked in at him through the windows of his private room.

The whole force of the blow had fallen on *him*. The share of his partners in the business was of the most trifling nature. The capital was his; the risk was his. Personally and privately, *he* had to find the money, or to confront the one other alternative – ruin.

How was the money to be found?

With his position in the City, he had only to go to the famous money-lending and discounting house of Bulpit Brothers – reported to 'turn over' millions in their business every year – and to supply himself at once with the necessary funds. Forty thousand pounds was a trifling transaction to Bulpit Brothers.

Having got the money, how, in the present state of his trade, was the loan to be paid back?

His thoughts reverted to his marriage with Natalie.

'Curious!' he said to himself, recalling his conversation with Sir Joseph on board the yacht. 'Graybrooke told me he would give his daughter half his fortune on her marriage. Half Graybrooke's fortune happens to be just forty thousand pounds!' He took a turn in the room. No! It was impossible to apply to Sir Joseph. Once shake Sir Joseph's conviction of his commercial solidity, and the marriage would be certainly deferred – if not absolutely broken off. Sir Joseph's fortune could be made available, in the present emergency, in but one way – he might use it to repay his debt. He had only to make the date at which the loan expired coincide with the date of his marriage, and there was his father-in-law's money at his disposal, or at his wife's disposal – which meant the same thing. 'It's well I pressed Graybrooke about the marriage when I did!' he thought. 'I can borrow the money at a short date. In three months from this Natalie will be my wife.'

He drove to his club, to get breakfast, with his mind cleared, for the time being, of all its anxieties but one.

Knowing where he could procure the loan, he was by no means equally sure of being able to find the security on which he could borrow the money. Living up to his income; having no expectations from any living creature; possessing in landed property only some thirty or forty acres in Somersetshire, with a quaint little dwelling, half-farmhouse, half-cottage, attached – he was incapable of providing the needful security from his own personal resources. To appeal to wealthy friends in the City would be to let those friends into the secret of his embarrassments, and to put his credit in peril. He finished his breakfast, and went back to Austin Friars – failing entirely, so far, to see how he was to remove the last obstacle now left in his way.

The doors were open to the public; business had begun. He had not been ten minutes in his room before the shipping-clerk knocked at the door and interrupted him, still absorbed in his own anxious thoughts.

'What is it?' he asked, irritably.

'Duplicate Bills of Lading, sir,' answered the clerk, placing the documents on his master's table.

Found! There was the security on his writing-desk, staring him in the face! He dismissed the clerk and examined the papers.

They contained an account of goods shipped to the London house, on board vessels sailing from Smyrna and Odessa, and they were signed by the masters of the ships, who thereby acknowledged the receipt of the goods, and undertook to deliver them safely to the persons owning them, as directed. First copies of these papers had already been placed in the possession of the London house. The duplicates had now followed, in case of accident. Richard Turlington instantly determined to make the duplicates serve as his security, keeping the first copies privately under lock and key, to be used in obtaining possession of the goods at the customary time. The fraud was a fraud in appearance only. The security was a pure formality. His marriage would supply him with the funds needed for repaying the money, and the profits of his business would provide, in course of time, for restoring the dowry of his wife. It was simply a question of preserving his credit by means which were legitimately at his disposal. Within the lax limits of mercantile morality, Richard Turlington had a conscience. He put on his hat and took his false security to the money-lenders, without feeling at all lowered in his own estimation as an honest man.

Bulpit Brothers, long desirous of having such a name as his on their books, received him with open arms. The security (covering the amount borrowed) was accepted as a matter of course. The money was lent, for three months, with a stroke of the pen. Turlington stepped out again into the street, and confronted the City of London in the character of the noblest work of mercantile creation – a solvent man.*

The Fallen Angel, walking invisibly behind, in Richard's shadow, flapped his crippled wings in triumph. From that moment the Fallen Angel had got him.

---

* It may not be amiss to remind the incredulous reader that a famous firm in the City accepted precisely the same security as that here accepted by Bulpit Brothers, with the same sublime indifference to troubling themselves by making any inquiry about it.

FOURTH SCENE

MUSWELL HILL

The next day Turlington drove to the suburbs, on the chance of finding the Graybrookes at home again. Sir Joseph disliked London, and could not prevail on himself to live any nearer to the metropolis than Muswell Hill. When Natalie wanted a change, and languished for balls, theatres, flower- shops, and the like, she had a room especially reserved for her in the house of Sir Joseph's married sister, Mrs Sancroft, living in that central deep of the fashionable whirlpool, known among mortals as Berkeley Square.

On his way through the streets, Turlington encountered a plain proof that the Graybrookes must have returned. He was passed by Launce, driving, in company with a gentleman, in a cab. The gentleman was Launce's brother, and the two were on their way to the Commissioner of Police to make the necessary arrangements for instituting an inquiry into Turlington's early life.

Arrived at the gate of the villa, the information received only partially fulfilled the visitor's expectations. The family had returned on the previous evening. Sir Joseph and his sister were at home, but Natalie was away again already. She had driven into town to lunch with her aunt.

Turlington went into the house.

'Have you lost any money?' Those were the first words uttered by Sir Joseph when he and Richard met again, after the parting on board the yacht.

'Not a farthing. I might have lost seriously, if I had not got back in time to set things straight. Stupidity on the part of my people left in charge – nothing more. It's all right now.'

Sir Joseph lifted his eyes, with heartfelt devotion, to the ceiling. 'Thank God, Richard!' he said, in tones of the deepest feeling. He rang the bell. 'Tell Miss Graybrooke Mr Turlington is here.' He turned again to Richard. 'Lavinia is like me – Lavinia has been so anxious about you. We have both of us passed a sleepless night.' Miss Lavinia came in. Sir Joseph hurried to meet her, and took her affectionately by both hands. 'My dear! the best of all good news, Richard has not lost a farthing.' Miss Lavinia lifted *her* eyes to the ceiling with heartfelt devotion, and said, 'Thank God, Richard!' – like the echo of her brother's voice; a little late, perhaps, for its reputation as an echo, but accurate to half a note in its perfect repetition of sound.

Turlington asked the question which it had been his one object to put in paying his visit to Muswell Hill.

'Have you spoken to Natalie?'

'This morning,' replied Sir Joseph. 'An opportunity offered itself after breakfast. I took advantage of it, Richard – you shall hear how.'

He settled himself in his chair for one of his interminable stories; he began his opening sentence – and stopped, struck dumb at the first word. There was an unexpected obstacle in the way – his sister was not attending to him; his sister had silenced him at starting. The story touching, this time, on the question of marriage, Miss Lavinia had her woman's interest in seeing full justice done to the subject. She seized on her brother's narrative as on property in her own right.

'Joseph should have told you,' she began, addressing herself to Turlington, 'that our dear girl was unusually depressed in spirits this morning. Quite in the right frame of mind for a little serious talk about her future life. She ate nothing at breakfast, poor child, but a morsel of dry toast.'

'And marmalade,' said Sir Joseph, striking in at the first opportunity. The story, on this occasion, being Miss Lavinia's story, the polite contradictions necessary to its successful progress were naturally transferred from the sister to the brother, and became contradictions on Sir Joseph's side.

'No,' said Miss Lavinia, gently, 'if you *will* have it, Joseph – jam.'

'I beg your pardon,' persisted Sir Joseph, 'marmalade.'

'What *does* it matter, brother?'

'Sister! the late great and good Doctor Johnson said accuracy ought always to be studied even in the most trifling things.'

'You *will* have your way, Joseph' – (this was the formula – answering to Sir Joseph's 'Let us waive the point' – which

Miss Lavinia used, as a means of conciliating her brother, and getting a fresh start for her story). 'Well, we took dear Natalie out between us, after breakfast, for a little walk in the grounds. My brother opened the subject with infinite delicacy and tact. "Circumstances," he said, "into which it was not then necessary to enter, made it very desirable, young as she was, to begin to think of her establishment in life." And then he referred, Richard (so nicely), to your faithful and devoted attachment——'

'Excuse me, Lavinia, I began with Richard's attachment, and then I got on to her establishment in life.'

'Excuse *me*, Joseph. You managed it much more delicately than you suppose. You didn't drag Richard in by the head and shoulders in that way.'

'Lavinia! I began with Richard.'

'Joseph! Your memory deceives you.'

Turlington's impatience broke through all restraint.

'How did it end?' he asked. 'Did you propose to her that we should be married in the first week of the New Year?'

'Yes!' said Miss Lavinia.

'No!' said Sir Joseph.

The sister looked at the brother, with an expression of affectionate surprise. The brother looked at the sister with a fund of amiable contradiction, expressed in a low bow.

'Do you really mean to deny, Joseph, that you told Natalie we had decided on the first week in the New Year?'

'I deny the New Year, Lavinia. I said early in January.'

'You *will* have your way, Joseph! We were walking in the shrubbery at the time. I had our dear girl's arm in mine, and I felt it tremble. She suddenly stopped. "Oh," she said, "not so soon!" I said, "My dear, consider Richard!" She turned to her father. She said, "Don't, pray don't press it so soon, papa! I respect Richard; I like Richard as your true and faithful friend; but I don't love him as I ought to love him if I am to be his wife." Imagine her talking in that way! What could she possibly know about it? Of course we both laughed——'

'*You* laughed, Lavinia.'

'*You* laughed, Joseph.'

'Get on, for God's sake!' cried Turlington, striking his hand passionately on the table by which he was sitting. 'Don't madden me by contradicting each other! Did she give way or not?'

Miss Lavinia turned to her brother. 'Contradicting each other, Joseph!' she exclaimed, lifting her hands in blank amazement.

'Contradicting each other!' repeated Sir Joseph, equally astonished on his side. 'My dear Richard, what can you be thinking of? I contradict my sister! We never disagreed in our lives.'

'I contradict my brother! We have never had a cross word between us from the time when we were children.'

Turlington internally cursed his own irritable temper.

'I beg your pardon – both of you,' he said. 'I didn't know what I was saying. Make some allowance for me. All my hopes in life are centred in Natalie; and you have just told me (in her own words, Miss Lavinia) that she doesn't love me. You don't mean any harm, I dare say; but you cut me to the heart.'

This confession, and the look that accompanied it, touched the ready sympathies of the two old people in the right place. The remainder of the story dropped between them by common consent. They vied with each other in saying the comforting words which would allay their dear Richard's anxiety. How little he knew of young girls. How could he be so foolish, poor fellow! as to attach any serious importance to what Natalie had said? As if a young creature in her teens knew the state of her own heart! Protestations and entreaties were matters of course, in such cases. Tears even might be confidently expected from a right-minded girl. It had all ended exactly as Richard would have wished it to end. Sir Joseph had said, 'My child! this is a matter of experience; love will come when you are married.' And Miss Lavinia had added, 'Dear Natalie, if you remembered your poor mother as I remember her, you would know that your father's experience is to be relied on.' In that way they had put it to her; and she had hung her head and had given – all that maiden modesty could be expected to give – a silent consent. 'The wedding-day was fixed for the first week in the

New Year. (No, Joseph; not January – the New Year.) And God bless you, Richard! and may your married life be a long and happy one.'

So the average ignorance of human nature, and the average belief in conventional sentiment, complacently contemplated the sacrifice of one more victim on the all-devouring altar of Marriage! So Sir Joseph and his sister provided Launcelot Linzie with the one argument which he wanted to convince Natalie: 'Choose between making the misery of your life by marrying *him*, and making the happiness of your life by marrying *me*.'

'When shall I see her?' asked Turlington, with Miss Lavinia (in tears which did *her* credit) in possession of one of his hands, and Sir Joseph (in tears which did *him* credit) in possession of the other.

'She will be back to dinner, dear Richard. Stay and dine.'

'Thank you. I must go into the City first. I will come back and dine.'

With that arrangement in prospect, he left them.

An hour later a telegram arrived from Natalie. She had consented to dine, as well as lunch, in Berkeley Square – sleeping there that night, and returning the next morning. Her father instantly telegraphed back by the messenger, insisting on Natalie's return to Muswell Hill that evening, in time to meet Richard Turlington at dinner.

'Quite right, Joseph,' said Miss Lavinia, looking over her brother's shoulder, while he wrote the telegram.

'She is showing a disposition to coquette with Richard,' rejoined Sir Joseph, with the air of a man who knew female human nature in its remotest corners. 'My telegram, Lavinia, will have its effect.'

Sir Joseph was quite right. His telegram *had* its effect. It not only brought his daughter back to dinner – it produced another result which his prophetic faculty had altogether failed to foresee.

The message reached Berkeley Square at five o'clock in the afternoon. Let us follow the message.

FIFTH SCENE

THE SQUARE

Between four and five in the afternoon – when the women of the western regions are in their carriages, and the men are at their clubs – London presents few places more conveniently adapted for purposes of private talk than the solitary garden enclosure of a Square.

On the day when Richard Turlington paid his visit to Muswell Hill, two ladies (with a secret between them) unlocked the gate of the railed garden in Berkeley Square. They shut the gate, after entering the enclosure, but carefully forbore to lock it as well, and carefully restricted their walk to the westward side of the garden. One of them was Natalie Graybrooke. The other was Mrs Sancroft's eldest daughter. A certain temporary interest attached, in the estimation of society, to this young lady. She had sold well in the marriage market. In other words, she had recently been raised to the position of Lord Winwood's second wife; his lordship conferring on the bride not only the honours of the peerage, but the additional distinction of being step-mother to his three single daughters, all older than herself. In person, Lady Winwood was little and fair. In character, she was dashing and resolute – a complete contrast to Natalie, and (on that very account) Natalie's bosom friend.

'My dear, one ambitious marriage in the family is quite enough! I have made up my mind that *you* shall marry the man you love. Don't tell me your courage is failing you – the excuse is contemptible; I decline to receive it. Natalie! the men have a phrase which exactly describes your character. You want back-bone!'

The bonnet of the lady who expressed herself in these peremptory terms barely reached the height of Natalie's shoulder. Natalie might have blown the little airy, light-haired, unsubstantial creature over the railings of the garden if she had taken a good long breath and stooped low enough. But who ever met with a tall woman who had a will of her own?

Natalie's languid brown eyes looked softly down in submissive attention from an elevation of five feet seven. Lady Winwood's brisk blue eyes looked brightly up in despotic command from an elevation of four feet eleven (in her shoes).

'You are trifling with Mr Linzie, my dear. Mr Linzie is a nice fellow. I like him. I won't have that.'

'Louisa!'

'Mr Turlington has nothing to recommend him. He is not a well-bred old gentleman of exalted rank. He is only an odious brute who happens to have made money. You shall *not* marry Mr Turlington. And you *shall* marry Launcelot Linzie.'

'Will you let me speak, Louisa?'

'I will let you answer – nothing more. Didn't you come crying to me this morning? Didn't you say, "Louisa, they have pronounced sentence on me! I am to be married in the first week of the New Year. Help me out of it, for Heaven's sake!" You said all that, and more. And what did I do when I had heard your story?'

'Oh, you were so kind——'

'Kind doesn't half express it. I have committed crimes on your account. I have deceived my husband and my mother. For your sake I got mamma to ask Mr Linzie to lunch (as *my* friend!). For your sake I have banished my unoffending husband, not an hour since, to his club. You wretched girl, who arranged a private conference in the library? Who sent Mr Linzie off to consult his friend in the Temple on the law of clandestine marriage? Who suggested your telegraphing home, and stopping here for the night? Who made an appointment to meet your young man privately in this detestable place in ten minutes' time? I did! I did! I did! All in your interests. All to prevent you from doing what I have done – marrying to please your family instead of to please yourself. (I don't complain, mind, of Lord Winwood, or of his daughters. *He* is charming; his daughters I shall tame in course of time. You are different. And Mr Turlington, as I observed before, is a brute.) Very well. Now what do you owe me on your side? You owe it to me at least to know your own mind. You don't know it. You coolly inform me that you daren't run the risk after all, and that you can't face the consequences on second thoughts. I'll tell you what! You don't deserve that nice fellow who worships the very ground you tread on. You are a bread-and-butter miss. I don't believe you are fond of him!'

'Not fond of him!' Natalie stopped, and clasped her hands in despair of finding language strong enough for the occasion. At the same moment the sound of a closing gate caught her ear. She looked round. Launce had kept his appointment before his time. Launce was in the garden, rapidly approaching them.

'Now for the Law of Clandestine Marriage!' said Lady Winwood. 'Mr Linzie, we will take it sitting.' She led the way to one of the benches in the garden, and placed Launce between Natalie and herself. 'Well, Chief Conspirator, have you got the License? No? Does it cost too much? Can I lend you the money?'

'It costs perjury, Lady Winwood, in my case,' said Launce. 'Natalie is not of age. I can only get a License by taking my oath that I marry her with her father's consent.' He turned piteously to Natalie. 'I couldn't very well do that,' he said, in the tone of a man who feels bound to make an apology, 'could I?' Natalie shuddered; Lady Winwood shrugged her shoulders.

'In your place a woman wouldn't have hesitated,' her ladyship remarked. 'But men are so selfish. Well? I suppose there is some other way?'

'Yes, there is another way,' said Launce. 'But there is a horrid condition attached to it——'

'Something worse than perjury, Mr Linzie? Murder?'

'I'll tell you directly, Lady Winwood. The marriage comes first. The condition follows. There is only one chance for us. We must be married by Banns.'

'Banns!' cried Natalie. 'Why, banns are publicly proclaimed in church!'

'They needn't be proclaimed in *your* church, you goose,' said Lady Winwood. 'And, even if they were, nobody would be the wiser. You may trust implicitly, my dear, in the elocution of an English clergyman!'

'That's just what my friend said,' cried Launce. '"Take a lodging near a large parish church, in a remote part of London," – (this is my friend's advice) – "go to the clerk, tell him you want to be married by Banns, and say you belong to that parish. As for the lady, in your place I should simplify it. I should say she belonged to the parish too. Give an address, and have some one there to answer questions. How is the clerk to know? He isn't likely to be over-anxious about it – his fee is eighteen-pence. The clerk makes his profit out of you, after you are married. The same rule applies to the parson. He will have your names supplied to him on a strip of paper, with dozens of other names; and he will read them out all together in one inarticulate jumble in church. You will stand at the altar when your time comes, with Brown and Jones, Nokes and Styles, Jack and Gill. All that you will have to do is, to take care that your young lady doesn't fall to Jack, and you to Gill, by mistake – and there you are, married by Banns." My friend's opinion, stated in his own words.'

Natalie sighed, and wrung her hands in her lap. 'We shall never get through it,' she said, despondingly.

Lady Winwood took a more cheerful view.

'I see nothing very formidable, as yet, my dear. But we have still to hear the end of it. You mentioned a condition just now, Mr Linzie.'

'I am coming to the condition, Lady Winwood. You naturally suppose, as I did, that I put Natalie into a cab, and run away with her from the church-door?'

'Certainly. And I throw an old shoe after you for luck, and go home again.'

Launce shook his head ominously.

'Natalie must go home again as well as you!'

Lady Winwood started. 'Is that the condition you mentioned just now?' she asked.

'That is the condition. I may marry her without anything serious coming of it. But, if I run away with her afterwards, and if you are there, aiding and abetting me, we are guilty of Abduction, and we may stand, side by side, at the bar of the Old Bailey to answer for it!'

Natalie sprang to her feet in horror. Lady Winwood held up one finger warningly, signing to her to let Launce go on.

'Natalie is not yet sixteen years old,' Launce proceeded. 'She must go straight back to her father's house from the church, and

I must wait to run away with her till her next birthday. When she's turned sixteen, she's ripe for elopement – not an hour before. There is the law of Abduction! Despotism in a free country – that's what I call it!'

Natalie sat down again with an air of relief.

'It's a very comforting law, *I* think,' she said. 'It doesn't force one to take the dreadful step of running away from home all at once. It gives one time to consider, and plan, and make up one's mind. I can tell you this, Launce, if I *am* to be persuaded into marrying you, the law of abduction is the only thing that will induce me to do it. You ought to thank the law, instead of abusing it.'

Launce listened – without conviction.

'It's a pleasant prospect,' he said, 'to part at the church-door, and to treat my own wife on the footing of a young lady who is engaged to marry another gentleman.'

'Is it any pleasanter for *me*,' retorted Natalie, 'to have Richard Turlington courting me, when I am all the time your wife? I shall never be able to do it. I wish I was dead!'

'Come! come!' interposed Lady Winwood. 'It's time to be serious. Natalie's birthday, Mr Linzie, is next Christmas Day. She will be sixteen——'

'At seven in the morning,' said Launce; 'I got that out of Sir Joseph. At one minute past seven, Greenwich mean-time, we may be off together. I got *that* out of the lawyer.'

'And it isn't an eternity to wait from now till Christmas Day. You get that, by way of completing the list of your acquisitions, out of *me*. In the mean time, can you, or can you not, manage to meet the difficulties in the way of the marriage?'

'I have settled everything,' Launce answered confidently. 'There is not a single difficulty left.'

He turned to Natalie, listening to him in amazement; and explained himself. It had struck him that he might appeal – with his purse in his hand, of course – to the interest felt in his affairs by the late stewardess of the yacht. That excellent woman had volunteered to do all that she could to help him. Her husband had obtained situations for his wife and himself on board another yacht – and they were both eager to assist in any conspiracy in which their late merciless master was destined to play the part of victim. When on shore, they lived in a populous London parish, far away from the fashionable district of Berkeley Square, and farther yet from the respectable suburb of Muswell Hill. A room in the house could be nominally engaged for Natalie, in the assumed character of the stewardess's niece – the stewardess undertaking to answer any purely formal questions which might be put by the Church authorities, and to be present at the marriage ceremony. As for Launce, he would actually, as well as nominally, live in the district close by; and the steward, if needful, would answer for *him*. Natalie might call at her parochial residence occasionally, under the wing of Lady Winwood; gaining leave of absence from Muswell Hill, on the plea of paying one of her customary visits at her aunt's house. The conspiracy, in brief, was arranged in all its details. Nothing was now wanting but the consent of the young lady; obtaining which, Launce would go to the parish church and give the necessary notice of a marriage by Banns on the next day. There was the plot. What did the ladies think of it?

Lady Winwood thought it perfect.

Natalie was not so easily satisfied.

'My father has always been so kind to me!' she said. 'The one thing I can't get over, Launce, is distressing papa. If he had been hard on me – as some fathers are – I shouldn't mind.' She suddenly brightened, as if she saw her position in a new light. 'Why should you hurry me?' she asked. 'I am going to dine at my aunt's to-day, and you are coming in the evening. Give me time! Wait till to-night.'

Launce instantly entered his protest against wasting a moment longer. Lady Winwood opened her lips to support him. They were both silenced at the same moment by the appearance of one of Mrs Sancroft's servants, opening the gate of the square.

Lady Winwood went forward to meet the man. A suspicion crossed her mind that he might be bringing bad news.

'What do you want?' she asked.

'I beg your pardon, my lady – the house-keeper said you were walking here with Miss Graybrooke. A telegram for Miss Graybrooke.'

Lady Winwood took the telegram from the man's hand; dismissed him, and went back with it to Natalie. Natalie opened it nervously. She read the message – and instantly changed. Her cheeks flushed deep; her eyes flashed with indignation. 'Even papa can be hard on me, it seems, when Richard asks him!' she exclaimed. She handed the telegram to Launce. Her eyes suddenly filled with tears. '*You* love me,' she said gently – and stopped. 'Marry me!' she added, with a sudden burst of resolution. 'I'll risk it!'

As she spoke those words, Lady Winwood read the telegram. It ran thus:–

'Sir Joseph Graybrooke, Muswell Hill. To Miss Natalie Graybrooke, Berkeley Square. Come back immediately. You are engaged to dine here with Richard Turlington.'

Lady Winwood folded up the telegram with a malicious smile. 'Well done, Sir Joseph!' thought her ladyship. 'We might never have persuaded Natalie – but for You!'

SIXTH SCENE

THE CHURCH

The time is morning; the date is early in the month of November. The place is a church, in a poor and populous parish in the undiscovered regions of London, eastward of the Tower, and hard by the riverside.

A marriage procession of five approaches the altar. The bridegroom is pale, and the bride is frightened. The bride's friend (a resolute-looking little lady) encourages her in whispers. The two respectable persons, apparently man and wife, who complete the procession, seem to be not quite clear as to the position which they occupy at the ceremony. The beadle, as he marshals them before the altar, sees something under the surface in this wedding-party. Marriages in the lower ranks of life are the only marriages celebrated here. Is this a runaway match? The beadle anticipates something out of the common, in the shape of a fee.

The clergyman (the junior curate) appears from the vestry in his robes. The clerk takes his place. The clergyman's eye rests with a sudden interest and curiosity on the bride and bridegroom, and on the bride's friend; notices the absence of elderly relatives; remarks, in the two ladies especially, evidences of refinement and breeding, entirely unparalleled in his professional experience of brides and brides' friends standing before the altar of that church; questions, silently and quickly, the eye of the clerk, occupied also in observing the strangers with interest. 'Jenkinson' (the clergyman's look asks), 'is this all right?' 'Sir' (the clerk's look answers), 'a marriage by banns; all the formalities have been observed.' The clergyman opens his book. The formalities have been observed; his duty lies plainly before him. Attention, Launcelot! Courage, Natalie! The service begins.

Launce casts a last furtive look round the church. Will Sir Joseph Graybrooke start up and stop it from one of the empty pews? Is Richard Turlington lurking in the organ loft, and only waiting till the words of the service appeal to him to prohibit the marriage, or 'else hereafter for ever to hold his peace?' No. The clergyman proceeds steadily, and nothing happens. Natalie's charming face grows paler and paler, Natalie's heart throbs faster and faster, as the time comes nearer for reading the words which unite them for life. Lady Winwood herself feels an unaccustomed fluttering in the region of the bosom. Her ladyship's thoughts revert, not altogether pleasantly, to her own marriage: 'Ah, me! what was *I* thinking of when I was in this position? Of the bride's beautiful dress, and of Lady Winwood's coming presentation at Court!'

The service advances to the words in which they plight their troth. Launce has put the Ring on her finger. Launce has repeated the words after the clergyman. Launce has married her! Done! Come what may of it, done!

The service ends. Bridegroom, bride, and witnesses go into the vestry to sign the book. The signing, like the service, is serious. No trifling with the truth is possible here. When it comes to Lady Winwood's turn, Lady Winwood must write her name. She does it, but without her usual grace and decision. She drops her handkerchief. The clerk picks it up for her, and notices that a coronet is embroidered in one corner.

The fees are paid. They leave the vestry. Other couples, when it is over, are talkative and happy. These two are more silent and more embarrassed than ever. Stranger still, while other couples go off with relatives and friends, all socially united in honour of the occasion, these two and their friends part at the church door. The respectable man and his wife go their way on foot. The little lady with the coronet on her handkerchief puts the bride into a cab, gets in herself, and directs the driver to close the door, while the bridegroom is standing on the church steps! The bridegroom's face is clouded, as well it may be. He puts his head in at the window of the cab; he possesses himself of the bride's hand; he speaks in a whisper; he is apparently not to be shaken off. The little lady exerts her authority, separates the clasped hands, pushes the bridegroom away, and cries peremptorily to the driver to go on. The cab starts; the deserted husband drifts desolately anyhow down the street. The clerk, who has seen it all, goes back to the vestry, and reports what has happened.

The rector (with his wife on his arm) has just dropped into the vestry on business in passing. He and the curate are talking about the strange marriage. The rector, gravely bent on ascertaining that no blame rests with the Church, interrogates, and is satisfied. The rector's wife is not so easy to deal with. She has looked at the signatures in the book. One of the names is familiar to her. She cross-examines the clerk as soon as her husband has done with him. When she hears of the coronet on the handkerchief she points to the signature of 'Louisa Winwood,' and says to the rector, 'I know who it is! Lord Winwood's second wife. I went to school with his lordship's daughters by his first marriage. We occasionally meet at the Sacred Concerts (on the "Ladies' Committee"); I shall find an opportunity of speaking to them. One moment, Mr Jenkinson, I will write down the names before you put away the book.

"Launcelot Linzie," "Natalie Graybrooke." Very pretty names; quite romantic. I do delight in a romance. Good-morning.'

She gives the curate a parting smile, and the clerk a parting nod, and sails out of the vestry. Natalie, silently returning in Lady Winwood's company to Muswell Hill; and Launce, cursing the law of abduction as he roams the streets – little think that the ground is already mined under their feet. Richard Turlington may hear of it now, or may hear of it later. The discovery of the marriage depends entirely on a chance meeting between the lord's daughters and the rector's wife.

SEVENTH SCENE

THE EVENING PARTY

> MR TURLINGTON
> LADY WINWOOD *At Home.*
> *Wednesday, December 15th – Ten o'clock.*

'DEAREST NATALIE, – As the brute insists, the brute must have the invitation which I enclose. Never mind, my child. You and Launce are coming to dinner, and I will see that you have your little private opportunities of retirement afterwards. All I expect of you in return is, *not* to look (when you come back) as if your husband had been kissing you. You will certainly let out the secret of those stolen kisses, if you don't take care. At mamma's dinner yesterday, your colour (when you came out of the conservatory) was a sight to see. Even your shoulders were red! They are charming shoulders, I know, and men take the strangest fancies sometimes. But, my dear, suppose you wear a chemisette next time, if you haven't authority enough over him to prevent his doing it again! – Your affectionate LOUISA.'

The private history of the days that had passed since the marriage was written in that letter. An additional chapter – of some importance in its bearing on the future – was contributed by the progress of events at Lady Winwood's party.

By previous arrangement with Natalie, the Graybrookes (invited to dinner) arrived early. Leaving her husband and her step-daughters to entertain Sir Joseph and Miss Lavinia, Lady Winwood took Natalie into her own boudoir, which communicated by a curtained opening with the drawing-room.

'My dear! you are looking positively haggard this evening. Has anything happened?'

'I am nearly worn out, Louisa. The life I am leading is so unendurable that, if Launce pressed me, I believe I should consent to run away with him when we leave your house to-night.'

'You will do nothing of the sort, if you please. Wait till you are sixteen. I delight in novelty, but the novelty of appearing at the Old Bailey is beyond my ambition. Is the brute coming to-night?'

'Of course. He insists on following me wherever I go. He lunched at Muswell Hill to-day. More complaints of my incomprehensible coldness to him. Another scolding from papa. A furious letter from Launce. If I let Richard kiss my hand again in his presence, Launce warns me he will knock him down. Oh, the meanness and the guiltiness of the life I am leading now! I am in the falsest of all false positions, Louisa, and you encouraged me to do it. I believe Richard Turlington suspects us. The last two times Launce and I tried to get a minute together at my aunt's, he contrived to put himself in our way. There he was, my dear, with his scowling face, looking as if he longed to kill Launce. Can you do anything for us to-night? Not on my account. But Launce is so impatient. If he can't say two words to me alone this evening, he declares he will come to Muswell Hill, and catch me in the garden to-morrow.'

'Compose yourself, my dear; he shall say his two words to-night.'

'How?'

Lady Winwood pointed through the curtained entrance of the boudoir to the door of the drawing-room. Beyond the door was the staircase landing. And beyond the landing was a second drawing-room, the smallest of the two.

'There are only three or four people coming to dinner,' her ladyship proceeded; 'and a few more in the evening. Being a small party, the small drawing-room will do for us. This drawing-room will not be lit, and there will be only my reading-lamp here in the boudoir. I shall give the signal for leaving the dining-room earlier than usual. Launce will join us before the evening-party begins. The moment he appears, send him in here – boldly before your aunt and all of us.'

'For what?'

'For your fan. Leave it there under the sofa-cushion before we go down to dinner. You will sit next to Launce, and you will give him private instructions not to find the fan. You will get impatient – you will go to find it yourself – and there you are. Take care of your shoulders, Mrs Linzie! I have nothing more to say.'

The guests asked to dinner began to arrive. Lady Winwood was recalled to her duties as mistress of the house.

It was a pleasant little dinner – with one drawback. It began too late. The ladies only reached the small drawing-room at ten minutes to ten. Launce was only able to join them as the clock struck.

'Too late!' whispered Natalie. 'He will be here directly.'

'Nobody comes punctually to an evening party,' said Launce. 'Don't let us lose a moment. Send me for your fan.'

Natalie opened her lips to say the necessary words. Before she could speak, the servant announced – 'Mr Turlington.'

He came in, with his stiffly-upright shirt collar and his loosely-fitting glossy black clothes. He made his sullen and clumsy bow to Lady Winwood. And then he did, what he had done dozens of times already – he caught Natalie, with her eyes still bright and her face still animated (after talking to Launce) – a striking contrast to the cold and unimpulsive young lady whom he was accustomed to see while Natalie was talking to *him*.

Lord Winwood's daughters were persons of some celebrity in the world of amateur music. Noticing the look that Turlington cast at Launce, Lady Winwood whispered to Miss Lavinia – who instantly asked the young ladies to sing. Launce, in obedience to a sign from Natalie, volunteered to find the music-books. It is needless to add that he pitched on the wrong volume at starting. As he lifted it from the piano to take it back to the stand, there dropped out from between the leaves a printed letter, looking like a circular. One of the young ladies took it up, and ran her eye over it, with a start.

'The Sacred Concerts!' she exclaimed.

Her two sisters, standing by, looked at each other guiltily: 'What will the Committee say to us? We entirely forgot the meeting last month.'

'Is there a meeting this month?'

They all looked anxiously at the printed letter.

'Yes! The twenty-third of December. Put it down in your book, Amelia.' Amelia, then and there, put it down among the engagements for the latter end of the month. And Natalie's unacknowledged husband placidly looked on.

So did the merciless irony of circumstances make Launce the innocent means of exposing his own secret to discovery. Thanks to his success in laying his hand on the wrong music-book, there would now be a meeting – two good days before the elopement could take place – between the lord's daughters and the rector's wife!

The guests of the evening began to appear by twos and threes. The gentlemen below-stairs left the dinner-table, and joined them. The small drawing-room was pleasantly filled, and no more. Sir Joseph Graybrooke, taking Turlington's hand, led him eagerly to their host. The talk in the dining-room had turned on finance. Lord Winwood was not quite satisfied with some of his foreign investments; and Sir Joseph's 'dear Richard' was the very man to give him a little sound advice. The three laid their heads together in a corner. Launce (watching them) slily pressed Natalie's hand. A renowned 'virtuoso' had arrived, and was thundering on the piano. The attention of the guests generally was absorbed in the performance. A fairer chance of sending Launce for the fan could not possibly have offered itself. While the financial discussion was still proceeding, the married lovers were ensconsed together, alone in the boudoir.

Lady Winwood (privately observant of their absence) kept her eye on the corner, watching Richard Turlington.

He was talking earnestly – with his back towards the company. He neither moved nor looked round. It came to Lord Winwood's turn to speak. He preserved the same position, listening. Sir Joseph took up the conversation next. Then his attention wandered – he knew beforehand what Sir Joseph would say. His eyes turned anxiously towards the place in which he had left Natalie. Lord Winwood said a word. His head turned back again towards the corner. Sir Joseph put an objection. He glanced once more over his shoulder – this time, at the place in which Launce had been standing. The next moment his host recalled his attention, and made it impossible for him to continue his scrutiny of the room. At the same time, two among the evening-guests, bound for another party, approached to take leave of the lady of the house. Lady Winwood was obliged to rise, and attend to them. They had something to say to her before they left, and they said it at terrible length; standing so as to intercept her view of the proceedings of the enemy. When she had got rid of them at last, she looked – and behold Lord Winwood and Sir Joseph were the only occupants of the corner!

Delaying one moment, to set the 'virtuoso' thundering once more, Lady Winwood slipped out of the room, and crossed the landing. At the entrance to the empty drawing-room she heard Turlington's voice, low and threatening, in the boudoir. Jealousy has a Second Sight of its own. He had looked in the right place at starting – and, oh heavens! he had caught them.

Her ladyship's courage was beyond dispute; but she turned pale, as she approached the entrance to the boudoir.

There stood Natalie – at once angry and afraid – between the man to whom she was ostensibly engaged, and the man to whom she was actually married. Turlington's rugged face expressed a martyrdom of suppressed fury. Launce – in the act of offering Natalie her fan – smiled, with the cool superiority of a man who knew that he had won his advantage, and who triumphed in knowing it.

'I forbid you to take your fan from that man's hands,' said Turlington, speaking to Natalie, and pointing to Launce.

'Isn't it rather too soon to begin "forbidding"?' asked Lady Winwood, good-humouredly.

'Exactly what I say!' exclaimed Launce. 'It seems necessary to remind Mr Turlington that he is not married to Natalie yet!'

Those last words were spoken in a tone which made both the women tremble inwardly for results. Lady Winwood took the fan from Launce with one hand, and took Natalie's arm with the other.

'There is your fan, my dear,' she said in her easy off-hand manner. 'Why do you allow these two barbarous men to keep you here while the great Bootmann is playing the Nightmare Sonata in the next room? Launce! Mr Turlington! follow me, and learn to be musical directly! You have only to shut your eyes, and you will fancy you hear four modern German composers playing, instead of one, and not the ghost of a melody among all the four.' She led the way out with Natalie, and whispered, 'Did he catch you?' Natalie whispered back, 'I heard him in time. He only caught us looking for the fan.' The two men waited behind to have two words together, alone in the boudoir.

'This doesn't end here, Mr Linzie!'

Launce smiled satirically. 'For once, I agree with you,' he answered. 'It doesn't end here, as you say.'

Lady Winwood stopped, and looked back at them from the drawing-room door. They were keeping her waiting – they had no choice but to follow the mistress of the house.

Arrived in the next room, both Turlington and Launce resumed their places among the guests with the same object in view. As a necessary result of the scene in the boudoir, each had his own special remonstrance to address to Sir Joseph. Even here, Launce was beforehand with Turlington. He was the first to get possession of Sir Joseph's private ear. His complaint took the form of a protest against Turlington's jealousy, and an appeal for a reconsideration of the sentence which excluded him from Muswell Hill. Watching them from a distance, Turlington's suspicious eye detected the appearance of something unduly confidential in the colloquy between the two. Under cover of the company, he stole behind them and listened.

The great Bootmann had arrived at that part of the Nightmare Sonata in which musical sound, produced principally with the left hand, is made to describe, beyond all possibility of mistake, the rising of the moon in a country churchyard, and a dance of Vampires round a maiden's grave. Sir Joseph, having no chance against the Vampires in a whisper, was obliged to raise his voice to make himself audible in answering and comforting Launce. 'I sincerely sympathize with you,' Turlington heard him say; 'and Natalie feels about it as I do. But Richard is an obstacle in our way. We must look to the consequences, my dear boy, supposing Richard found us out.' He nodded kindly to his nephew; and, declining to pursue the subject, moved away to another part of the room.

Turlington's jealous distrust, wrought to the highest pitch of irritability for weeks past, instantly associated the words he had just heard with the words spoken by Launce in the boudoir, which had reminded him that he was not married to Natalie yet. Was there treachery at work under the surface? and was the object to persuade weak Sir Joseph to reconsider his daughter's contemplated marriage in a sense favourable to Launce? Turlington's blind suspicion over-leapt at a bound all the manifest improbabilities which forbade such a conclusion as this. After an instant's consideration with himself, he decided on keeping his own counsel, and on putting Sir Joseph's good faith then and there to a test which he could rely on as certain to take Natalie's father by surprise.

'Graybrooke!'

Sir Joseph started at the sight of his future son-in-law's face.

'My dear Richard, you are looking very strangely! Is the heat of the room too much for you?'

'Never mind the heat! I have seen enough to-night to justify me in insisting that your daughter and Launcelot Linzie shall meet no more between this and the day of my marriage.' Sir

Joseph attempted to speak. Turlington declined to give him the opportunity. 'Yes! yes! your opinion of Linzie isn't mine, I know. I saw you as thick as thieves together just now.' Sir Joseph once more attempted to make himself heard. Wearied by Turlington's perpetual complaints of his daughter and his nephew, he was sufficiently irritated by this time to have reported what Launce had actually said to him if he had been allowed the chance. But Turlington persisted in going on. 'I cannot prevent Linzie from being received in this house, and at your sister's,' he said; 'but I can keep him out of *my* house in the country, and to the country let us go. I propose a change in the arrangements. Have you any engagement for the Christmas holidays?'

He paused, and fixed his eyes attentively on Sir Joseph. Sir Joseph, looking a little surprised, replied briefly that he had no engagement.

'In that case,' resumed Turlington, 'I invite you all to Somersetshire, and I propose that the marriage shall take place from my house, and not from yours. Do you refuse?'

'It is contrary to the usual course of proceeding in such cases, Richard,' Sir Joseph began.

'Do you refuse?' reiterated Turlington. 'I tell you plainly, I shall place a construction of my own upon your motive if you do.'

'No, Richard,' said Sir Joseph quietly, 'I accept.'

Turlington drew back a step in silence. Sir Joseph had turned the tables on him, and had taken *him* by surprise.

'It will upset several plans, and be strongly objected to by the ladies,' proceeded the old gentleman. 'But if nothing less will satisfy you, I say, Yes! I shall have occasion when we meet to-morrow at Muswell Hill to appeal to your indulgence under circumstances which may greatly astonish you. The least I can do in the mean time is to set an example of friendly sympathy and forbearance on my side. No more now, Richard. Hush! the music!'

It was impossible to make him explain himself further that night. Turlington was left to interpret Sir Joseph's mysterious communication with such doubtful aid to success as his own unassisted ingenuity might afford.

The meeting of the next day at Muswell Hill had for its object – as Turlington had already been informed – the drawing of Natalie's marriage settlement. Was the question of money at the bottom of Sir Joseph's contemplated appeal to his indulgence? He thought of his commercial position. The depression in the Levant trade still continued. Never had his business at any previous time required such constant attention, and repaid that attention with so little profit. The Bills of Lading had been already used by the firm, in the ordinary course of trade, to obtain possession of the goods. The duplicates in the hands of Bulpit Brothers were literally waste paper. Repayment of the loan of forty thousand pounds (with interest) was due in less than a month's time. There was his commercial position! Was it possible that money-loving Sir Joseph had any modification to propose in the matter of his daughter's dowry? The bare dread that it might be so, struck him cold. He quitted the house – and forgot to wish Natalie good-night.

Meanwhile, Launce had left the evening party before him – and Launce also found matter for serious reflection presented to his mind before he slept that night. In other words, he found, on reaching his lodgings, a letter from his brother, marked 'private.' Had the inquiry into the secrets of Turlington's early life – now prolonged over some weeks – led to positive results at last? Launce eagerly opened the letter. It contained a Report and a Summary. He passed at once to the Summary, and read these words:

'If you only want moral evidence to satisfy your own mind, your end is gained. There is, morally, no doubt that Turlington and the sea captain who cast the foreign sailor overboard to drown, are one and the same man. Legally, the matter is beset by difficulties, Turlington having destroyed all provable connection between his present self and his past life. There is only one chance for us. A sailor on board the ship (who was in his master's secrets) is supposed to be still living (under his master's protection). All the black deeds of Turlington's early life are known to this man. He can prove the facts, if we can find him, and make it worth his while to speak. Under what *alias* he is hidden we do not know. His own name is Thomas Wildfang. If we are to make the attempt to find him, not a moment is to be lost. The expenses may be serious. Let me know whether we are to go on, or whether enough has been done to attain the end you have in view.'

Enough had been done − not only to satisfy Launce, but to produce the right effect on Sir Joseph's mind if Sir Joseph proved obdurate when the secret of the marriage was revealed. Launce wrote a line directing the stoppage of the proceedings at the point which they had now reached. 'Here is a reason for her not marrying Turlington,' he said to himself, as he placed the papers under lock and key. 'And if she doesn't marry Turlington,' he added, with a lover's logic, 'why shouldn't she marry Me?'

EIGHTH SCENE

THE LIBRARY

The next day Sir Joseph Graybrooke, Sir Joseph's lawyer, Mr Dicas (highly respectable and immensely rich), and Richard Turlington were assembled in the library at Muswell Hill, to discuss the question of Natalie's marriage settlement.

After the usual preliminary phrases had been exchanged, Sir Joseph showed some hesitation in openly approaching the question which the little party of three had met to debate. He avoided his lawyer's eye; and he looked at Turlington rather uneasily.

'Richard,' he began at last, 'when I spoke to you about your marriage, on board the yacht, I said I would give my daughter——' Either his courage or his breath failed him at that point. He was obliged to wait a moment before he could go on.

'I said I would give my daughter half my fortune on her marriage,' he resumed. 'Forgive me, Richard. I can't do it!'

Mr Dicas, waiting for his instructions, laid down his pen, and looked at Sir Joseph's son-in-law elect. What would Mr Turlington say?

He said nothing. Sitting opposite the window, he rose when Sir Joseph spoke, and placed himself at the other side of the table, with his back to the light.

'My eyes are weak this morning,' he said, in an unnaturally low tone of voice. 'The light hurts them.'

He could find no more plausible excuse than that for concealing his face in shadow from the scrutiny of the two men on either side of him. The continuous moral irritation of his unhappy courtship – a courtship which had never advanced beyond the frigid familiarity of kissing Natalie's hand in the presence of others – had physically deteriorated him. Even *his* hardy nerves began to feel the long strain of suspicion that had been laid unremittingly on them for weeks past. His power of self-control – he knew it himself – was not to be relied on. He could hide his face: he could no longer command it.

'Did you hear what I said, Richard?'

'I heard. Go on.'

Sir Joseph proceeded, gathering confidence as he advanced.

'Half my fortune!' he repeated. 'It's parting with half my life; it's saying good-bye for ever to my dearest friend! My money has been such a comfort to me, Richard; such a pleasant occupation for my mind. I know no reading so interesting and so instructive as the reading of one's Banker's Book. To watch the outgoings on one side,' said Sir Joseph, with a gentle and pathetic solemnity, 'and the incomings on the other – the sad lessening of the balance at one time, and the cheering and delightful growth of it at another – what absorbing reading! The best novel that ever was written isn't to be mentioned in a breath with it. I cannot, Richard, I really can *not*, see my nice round balance shrink up to half the figure that I have been used to for a life-time. It may be weak of me,' proceeded Sir Joseph, evidently feeling that it was not weak of him at all, 'but we all have our tender place, and my Banker's Book is mine. Besides, it isn't as if you wanted it. If you wanted it, of course—— But you don't want it. You are a rich man; you are marrying my dear Natalie for love, not for money. You and she and my grandchildren will have it all at my death. It *can* make no difference to you to wait a few years till the old man's chair at the fireside is empty. Will you say the fourth part, Richard, instead of the half? Twenty thousand,' pleaded Sir Joseph, piteously. 'I can bear twenty thousand off. For God's sake don't ask me for more!'

The lips of the lawyer twisted themselves sourly into an ironical smile. He was quite as fond of his money as Sir Joseph. He ought to have felt for his client; but rich men have no sympathy with one another. Mr Dicas openly despised Sir Joseph.

There was a pause. The robin-redbreasts in the shrubbery outside must have had prodigious balances at their bankers; they hopped up on the window-sill so fearlessly; they looked in with so little respect at the two rich men.

'Don't keep me in suspense, Richard,' proceeded Sir Joseph. 'Speak out. Is it yes or no?'

Turlington struck his hand excitedly on the table, and burst out on a sudden with the answer which had been so strangely delayed.

'Twenty thousand with all my heart!' he said. 'On this condition, Graybrooke, that every farthing of it is settled on Natalie, and on her children after her. Not a halfpenny to me!' he cried magnanimously, in his brassiest tones. 'Not a halfpenny to me!'

Let no man say the rich are heartless. Sir Joseph seized his son-in-law's hand in silence, and burst into tears.

Mr Dicas, habitually a silent man, uttered the first two words that had escaped him since the business began. 'Highly creditable,' he said, and took a note of his instructions on the spot.

From that point the business of the settlement flowed smoothly on to its destined end. Sir Joseph explained his views at the fullest length, and the lawyer's pen kept pace with him. Turlington, remaining in his place at the table, restricted himself to a purely passive part in the proceedings. He answered briefly when it was absolutely necessary to speak, and he agreed with the two elders in everything. A man has no attention to place at the disposal of other people when he stands at a crisis in his life. Turlington stood at that crisis, at the trying moment when Sir Joseph's unexpected proposal pressed instantly for a reply. Two merciless alternatives confronted him. Either he must repay the borrowed forty thousand pounds on the day when repayment was due, or he must ask Bulpit Brothers to grant him an extension of time, and so inevitably provoke an examination into the fraudulent security deposited with the firm, which could end in but one way. His last, literally his last chance, after Sir Joseph had diminished the promised dowry by one half, was to adopt the high-minded tone which became his position, and to conceal the truth until he could reveal it to his father-in-law in the privileged character of Natalie's husband. 'I owe forty thousand pounds, sir, in a fortnight's time, and I have not got a farthing of my own. Pay for me, or you will see your son-in-law's name in the Bankrupt's List.' For his daughter's sake – who could doubt it? – Sir Joseph would produce the money. The one thing needful was to be married in time. If either by accident or treachery Sir Joseph was led into deferring the appointed day, by so much as a fortnight only, the fatal 'call' would come, and the firm of Pizzituti, Turlington, and Branca would appear in the Gazette.

So he reasoned, standing on the brink of the terrible discovery which was soon to reveal to him that Natalie was the wife of another man.

'Richard!'

'Mr Turlington!'

He started, and roused his attention to present things. Sir Joseph on one side, and the lawyer on the other, were both appealing to him, and both regarding him with looks of amazement.

'Have you done with the settlement?' he asked.

'My dear Richard, we have done with it long since,' replied Sir Joseph. 'Have you really not heard what I have been saying for the last quarter of an hour to good Mr Dicas here? What *can* you have been thinking of?'

Turlington did not attempt to answer the question. 'Am I interested,' he asked, 'in what you have been saying to Mr Dicas?'

'You shall judge for yourself,' answered Sir Joseph, mysteriously; 'I have been giving Mr Dicas his instructions for making my Will. I wish the Will and the Marriage Settlement to be executed at the same time. Read the instructions, Mr Dicas.'

Sir Joseph's contemplated Will proved to have two merits – it was simple and it was short. Excepting one or two trifling legacies to distant relatives, he had no one to think of (Miss Lavinia being already provided for) but his daughter and the children who might be born of her marriage. In its various provisions, made with these two main objects in view, the Will followed the precedents established in such cases. It differed in no important respect from the tens of thousands of other wills made under similar circumstances. Sir Joseph's motive in claiming special attention for it still remained unexplained, when Mr Dicas reached the clause devoted to the appointment of executors and trustees; and announced that this portion of the document was left in blank.

'Sir Joseph Graybrooke, are you prepared to name the persons whom you appoint?' asked the lawyer.

Sir Joseph rose, apparently for the purpose of giving special importance to the terms in which he answered his lawyer's question.

'I appoint,' he said, 'as sole executor and trustee – Richard Turlington.'

It was no easy matter to astonish Mr Dicas. Sir Joseph's reply absolutely confounded him. He looked across the table at his client and delivered himself on this special occasion of as many as three words.

'Are you mad?' he asked.

Sir Joseph's healthy complexion slightly reddened. 'I never was in more complete possession of myself, Mr Dicas, than at this moment.'

Mr Dicas was not to be silenced in that way.

'Are you aware of what you do,' persisted the lawyer, 'if you appoint Mr Turlington as the sole executor and trustee? You put it in the power of your daughter's husband, sir, to make away with every farthing of your money after your death.'

Turlington had hitherto listened with an appearance of interest in the proceedings, which he assumed as an act of politeness. To his view, the future was limited to the date at which Bulpit Brothers had a right to claim the repayment of their loan. The Will was a matter of no earthly importance to him, by comparison with the infinitely superior interest of the Marriage. It was only when the lawyer's brutally plain language forced his attention to it, that the question of his pecuniary interest in his father-in-law's death assumed its fit position in his mind.

His colour rose; and *he* too showed that he was offended by what Mr Dicas had just said.

'Not a word, Richard! Let me speak for you as well as for myself,' said Sir Joseph. 'For seven years past,' he continued, turning to the lawyer, 'I have been accustomed to place the most unlimited trust in Richard Turlington. His disinterested advice has enabled me largely to increase my income, without placing a farthing of the principal in jeopardy. On more than one occasion, I have entreated him to make use of my money in his business. He has invariably refused to do so. Even his bitterest enemies, sir, have been obliged to acknowledge that my interests were safe when committed to his care. Am I to begin distrusting him, now that I am about to give him my daughter in marriage? Am I to leave it on record that I doubt him for the first time – when my Will is opened after my death? No! I can confide the management of the fortune which my child will inherit after me, to no more competent or more honourable hands than the hands of the man who is to marry her. I maintain my appointment, Mr Dicas! I persist in placing the whole responsibility under my Will in my son-in-law's care.'

Turlington attempted to speak. The lawyer attempted to speak. Sir Joseph – with a certain simple dignity which had its effect on both of them – declined to hear a word on either side. 'No, Richard! as long as I am alive this is my business, not yours. No, Mr Dicas! I understand that it is your business to protest professionally. You have protested. Fill in the blank space as I have told you. Or leave the instructions on the table, and I will send for the nearest solicitor to complete them in your place.'

Those words placed the lawyer's position plainly before him. He had no choice but to do as he was bid, or to lose a good client. He did as he was bid, and grimly left the room.

Sir Joseph, with old-fashioned politeness, followed him as far as the hall. Returning to the library to say a few friendly words before finally dismissing the subject of the Will, he found himself seized by the arm, and dragged without ceremony, in Turlington's powerful grasp, to the window.

'Richard!' he exclaimed, 'what does this mean?'

'Look!' cried the other, pointing through the window to a grassy walk in the grounds, bounded on either side by shrubberies, and situated at a little distance from the house. 'Who is that man? – quick! before we lose sight of him – the man crossing there from one shrubbery to the other?' Sir Joseph failed to recognize the figure before it disappeared. Turlington whispered fiercely, close to his ear – 'Launcelot Linzie!'

In perfect good faith Sir Joseph declared that the man could not possibly have been Launce. Turlington's frenzy of jealous suspicion was not to be so easily calmed. He asked significantly for Natalie. She was reported to be walking in the grounds. 'I knew it!' he said, with an oath – and hurried out into the grounds to discover the truth for himself.

Some little time elapsed before he came back to the house. He had discovered Natalie – alone. Not a sign of Launce had rewarded his search. For the hundredth time he had offended Natalie. For the hundredth time he was compelled to appeal to the indulgence of her father and her aunt. 'It won't happen again,' he said, sullenly penitent. 'You will find me quite another man when I have got you all at my house in the country. Mind!' he burst out, with a furtive look, which expressed his inveterate distrust of Natalie and of every one about her. 'Mind! it's settled that you all come to me in Somersetshire, on Monday next.' Sir Joseph answered rather drily that it *was* settled. Turlington turned to leave the room –

and suddenly came back. 'It's understood,' he went on, addressing Miss Lavinia, 'that the seventh of next month is the date fixed for the marriage. Not a day later!' Miss Lavinia replied rather drily, on her side, 'Of course, Richard; not a day later.' He muttered, 'All right' – and hurriedly left them.

Half an hour afterwards Natalie came in, looking a little confused.

'Has he gone?' she asked, whispering to her aunt.

Relieved on this point, she made straight for the library – a room which she rarely entered, at that, or any other period of the day. Miss Lavinia followed her, curious to know what it meant. Natalie hurried to the window, and waved her handkerchief – evidently making a signal to some one outside. Miss Lavinia instantly joined her, and took her sharply by the hand.

'Is it possible, Natalie?' she asked. 'Has Launcelot Linzie really been here, unknown to your father or to me?'

'Where is the harm if he was?' answered Natalie, with a sudden outbreak of temper. 'Am I never to see my cousin again, because Mr Turlington happens to be jealous of him?'

She suddenly turned away her head. The rich colour flowed over her face and neck. Miss Lavinia, proceeding sternly with the administration of the necessary reproof, was silenced midway by a new change in her niece's variable temper. Natalie burst into tears. Satisfied with this appearance of sincere contrition, the old lady consented to overlook what had happened; and, for this occasion only, to keep her niece's secret. They would all be in Somersetshire, she remarked, before any more breaches of discipline could be committed. Richard had fortunately made no discoveries; and the matter might safely be trusted, all things considered, to rest where it was.

Miss Lavinia might possibly have taken a less hopeful view of the circumstances, if she had known that one of the men-servants at Muswell Hill was in Richard Turlington's pay – and that this servant had seen Launce leave the grounds by the back garden gate.

NINTH SCENE

THE DRAWING-ROOM

'Amelia!'

'Say something.'

'Ask him to sit down.'

Thus addressing one another in whispers, the three step-daughters of Lady Winwood stood bewildered in their own drawing-room, helplessly confronting an object which appeared before them on the threshold of the door.

The date was the 23rd of December. The time was between two and three in the afternoon. The occasion was the return of the three sisters from the Committee meeting of the Sacred Concerts' Society. And the object was Richard Turlington.

He stood hat in hand at the door, amazed by his reception. 'I have come up this morning from Somersetshire,' he said. 'Haven't you heard? A matter of business at the office has forced me to leave my guests at my house in the country. I return to them to-morrow. When I say my guests, I mean the Graybrookes. Don't you know they are staying with me? Sir Joseph and Miss Lavinia and Natalie——?' On the utterance of Natalie's name, the sisters roused themselves. They turned about and regarded each other with looks of dismay. Turlington's patience began to fail him. 'Will you be so good as to tell me what all this means?' he said, a little sharply. 'Miss Lavinia asked me to call here when she heard I was coming to town. I was to take charge of a pattern for a dress, which she said you would give me. You ought to have received a telegram explaining it all, hours since. Has the message not reached you?'

The leading spirit of the three sisters was Miss Amelia. She was the first who summoned presence of mind enough to give a plain answer to Turlington's plain question.

'We received the telegram this morning,' she said. 'Something has happened since which has shocked and surprised us. We beg your pardon.' She turned to one of her sisters. 'Sophia, the pattern is ready in the drawer of that table behind you. Give it to Mr Turlington.'

Sophia produced the packet. Before she handed it to the visitor, she looked at her sister. 'Ought we to let Mr Turlington go,' she asked, 'as if nothing had happened?'

Amelia considered silently with herself. Dorothea, the third sister (who had not spoken yet), came forward with a suggestion. She proposed, before proceeding further, to inquire whether Lady Winwood was in the house. The idea was instantly adopted. Sophia rang the bell. Amelia put the questions when the servant appeared.

Lady Winwood had left the house for a drive immediately after luncheon. Lord Winwood — inquired for next — had accompanied her ladyship. No message had been left indicating the hour of their return.

The sisters looked at Turlington, uncertain what to say or do next. Miss Amelia addressed him as soon as the servant had left the room.

'Is it possible for you to remain here until either my father or Lady Winwood return?' she asked.

'It is quite impossible. Minutes are of importance to me to-day.'

'Will you give us one of your minutes? We want to consider something which we may have to say to you before you go.'

Turlington, wondering, took a chair. Miss Amelia put the case before her sisters from the sternly conscientious point of view, at the opposite end of the room.

'We have not found out this abominable deception by any underhand means,' she said. 'The discovery has been forced upon us, and we stand pledged to nobody to keep the secret. Knowing as we do how cruelly this gentleman has been used, it seems to me that we are bound in honour to open his eyes to the truth. If we remain silent we make ourselves Lady Winwood's accomplices. I, for one — I don't care what may come of it — refuse to do that.'

Her sisters agreed with her. The first chance their clever stepmother had given them of asserting their importance against hers was now in their hands. Their jealous hatred of Lady Winwood assumed the mask of Duty — duty towards an outraged and deceived fellow-creature. Could any earthly motive be purer than that? 'Tell him, Amelia!' cried the two young ladies, with the headlong recklessness of the sex which only stops to think when the time for reflection has gone by.

A vague sense of something wrong began to stir uneasily in Turlington's mind.

'Don't let me hurry you,' he said, 'but if you really have anything to tell me——'

Miss Amelia summoned her courage, and began.

'We have something very dreadful to tell you,' she said, interrupting him. 'You have been presented in this house, Mr Turlington, as a gentleman engaged to marry Lady Winwood's cousin, Miss Natalie Graybrooke.' She paused there – at the outset of the disclosure. A sudden change of expression passed over Turlington's face, which daunted her for the moment. 'We have hitherto understood,' she went on, 'that you were to be married to that young lady early in next month.'

'Well?'

He could say that one word. Looking at their pale faces, and their eager eyes, he could say no more.

'Take care!' whispered Dorothea, in her sister's ear. 'Look at him, Amelia! Not too soon.'

Amelia went on more carefully.

'We have just returned from a musical meeting,' she said. 'One of the ladies there was an acquaintance, a former school-fellow of ours. She is the wife of the rector of St Columb Major – a large church, far from this – at the East-end of London.'

'I know nothing about the woman or the church,' interposed Turlington, sternly.

'I must beg you to wait a little. I can't tell you what I want to tell you unless I refer to the rector's wife. She knows Lady Winwood by name. And she heard of Lady Winwood recently under very strange circumstances – circumstances connected with a signature in one of the books of the church.'

Turlington lost his self-control. 'You have got something against my Natalie,' he burst out; 'I know it by your whispering, I see it in your looks! Say it at once in plain words.'

There was no trifling with him now. In plain words Amelia said it.

* * * * * *

There was silence in the room. They could hear the sound of passing footsteps in the street. He stood perfectly still on the spot where they had struck him dumb by the disclosure, supporting himself with his right hand laid on the head of a sofa near him. The sisters drew back horror-struck into the farthest corner of the room. His face turned them cold. Through the mute misery which it had expressed at first, there appeared, slowly forcing its way to view, a look of deadly vengeance which froze them to the soul. They whispered feverishly one to the other, without knowing what they were talking of, without hearing their own voices. One of them said, 'Ring the bell!' Another said, 'Offer him something, he will faint.' The third shuddered, and repeated, over and over again, 'Why did we do it? Why did we do it?'

He silenced them on the instant by speaking on his side. He came on slowly, by a step at a time, with the big drops of agony falling slowly over his rugged face. He said, in a hoarse whisper, 'Write me down the name of the church – there.' He held out his open pocket-book to Amelia, while he spoke. She steadied herself, and wrote the address. She tried to say a word to soften him. The word died on her lips. There was a light in his eyes as they looked at her, which transfigured his face to something superhuman and devilish. She turned away from him, shuddering.

He put the book back in his pocket, and passed his handkerchief over his face. After a moment of indecision, he suddenly and swiftly stole out of the room, as if he was afraid of their calling somebody in, and stopping him. At the door he turned round for a moment, and said, 'You will hear how this ends. I wish you good morning.'

The door closed on him. Left by themselves, they began to realize it. They thought of the consequences when his back was turned and it was too late.

The Graybrookes! Now he knew it, what would become of the Graybrookes? What would he do when he got back? Even at ordinary times – when he was on his best behaviour – he was a rough man. What would happen? Oh, good God! what would happen when he and Natalie next stood face to face? It was a lonely house – Natalie had told them about it – no neighbours near; nobody by to interfere but the weak old father and the maiden aunt. Something ought to be done. Some steps ought to be taken to warn them. Advice – who could give advice? Who was the first person who ought to be told of what had happened? Lady Winwood? No! even at that crisis the sisters still shrank from their stepmother – still hated her with the old hatred! Not a word to *her*! They owed no duty to *her*! Who else could they appeal to? To their father? Yes! There was the person to advise them. In the meanwhile, silence towards their stepmother – silence towards everyone till their father came back!

They waited and waited. One after another the precious hours, pregnant with the issues of life and death, followed each other on the dial. Lady Winwood returned alone. She had left her husband at the House of Lords. Dinner-time came, and brought with it a note from his lordship. There was a Debate at the House. Lady Winwood and his daughters were not to wait dinner for him.

TENTH SCENE

GREEN ANCHOR LANE

An hour later than the time at which he had been expected, Richard Turlington appeared at his office in the city.

He met beforehand all the inquiries which the marked change in him must otherwise have provoked, by announcing that he was ill. Before he proceeded to business, he asked if anybody was waiting to see him. One of the servants from Muswell Hill was waiting with another parcel for Miss Lavinia, ordered by telegram from the country that morning. Turlington (after ascertaining the servant's name) received the man in his private room. He there heard, for the first time, that Launcelot Linzie had been lurking in the grounds (exactly as he had supposed) on the day when the lawyer took his instructions for the Settlement and the Will.

In two hours more Turlington's work was completed. On leaving the office — as soon as he was out of sight of the door — he turned eastward, instead of taking the way that led to his own house in town. Pursuing his course, he entered the labyrinth of streets which led, in that quarter of East London, to the unsavoury neighbourhood of the river side.

By this time his mind was made up. The forecast shadow of meditated crime travelled before him already, as he threaded his way among his fellow-men.

He had been to the vestry of St Columb Major, and had satisfied himself that he was misled by no false report. There was the entry in the Marriage Register. The one unexplained mystery was the mystery of Launce's conduct in permitting his wife to return to her father's house. Utterly unable to account for this proceeding, Turlington could only accept facts as they were, and determine to make the most of his time, while the woman who had deceived him was still under his roof. A hideous expression crossed his face as he realized the idea that he had got her (unprotected by her husband) in his house. 'When Launcelot Linzie *does* come to claim her,' he said to himself, 'he shall find I have been even with him.' He looked at his watch. Was it possible to save the last train and get back that night? No — the last train had gone. Would she take advantage of his absence to escape? He had little fear of it. She would never have allowed her aunt to send him to Lord Winwood's house, if she had felt the slightest suspicion of his discovering the truth in that quarter. Returning by the first train the next morning, he might feel sure of getting back in time. Meanwhile, he had the hours of the night before him. He could give his mind to the serious question that must be settled before

he left London – the question of repaying the forty thousand
pounds. There was but one way of getting the money now. Sir
Joseph had executed his Will; Sir Joseph's death would leave his
sole executor and trustee (the lawyer had said it!) master of his
fortune. Turlington determined to be master of it in four-and-
twenty hours – striking the blow, without risk to himself, by
means of another hand. In the face of the probabilities, in the
face of the facts, he had now firmly persuaded himself that Sir
Joseph was privy to the fraud that had been practised on him.
The Marriage Settlement, the Will, the presence of the family at
his country house – all these he believed to be so many
stratagems invented to keep him deceived until the last
moment. The truth was in those words which he had overheard
between Sir Joseph and Launce – and in Launce's presence
(privately encouraged, no doubt) at Muswell Hill. 'Her father
shall pay me for it doubly: with his purse and with his life.'
With that thought in his heart, Richard Turlington wound his
way through the streets by the river side, and stopped at a blind
alley called Green Anchor Lane, infamous to this day as the
chosen resort of the most abandoned wretches whom London
can produce.

The policeman at the corner cautioned him as he turned into
the alley. 'They won't hurt *me*!' he answered, and walked on to
a public house at the bottom of the lane.

The landlord at the door silently recognized him, and led the
way in. They crossed a room filled with sailors of all nations
drinking; ascended a staircase at the back of the house, and
stopped at the door of a room on the second floor. There, the
landlord spoke for the first time. 'He has outrun his allowance,
sir, as usual. You will find him with hardly a rag on his back. I
doubt if he will last much longer. He had another fit of the
horrors last night, and the doctor thinks badly of him.' With
that introduction he opened the door, and Turlington entered
the room.

On the miserable bed lay a grey-headed old man, of
gigantic stature, with nothing on him but a ragged shirt and a
pair of patched filthy trousers. At the side of the bed, with a
bottle of gin on the ricketty table between them, sat two

hideous, leering, painted monsters, wearing the dress of women. The smell of opium was in the room, as well as the smell of spirits. At Turlington's appearance, the old man rose on the bed and welcomed him with greedy eyes and outstretched hand.

'Money, master!' he called out hoarsely. 'A crown piece in advance, for the sake of old times!'

Turlington turned to the women without answering, purse in hand.

'His clothes are at the pawnbroker's, of course. How much?'

'Thirty shillings.'

'Bring them here, and be quick about it. You will find it worth your while when you come back.'

The women took the pawnbroker's tickets from the pockets of the man's trousers and hurried out.

Turlington closed the door, and seated himself by the bedside. He laid his hand familiarly on the giant's mighty shoulder; looked him full in the face, and said in a whisper:–

'Thomas Wildfang!'

The man started, and drew his huge hairy hand across his eyes, as if in doubt whether he was waking or sleeping. 'It's better than ten years, master, since you called me by my name. If I am Thomas Wildfang, what are You?'

'Your captain, once more.'

Thomas Wildfang sat up on the side of the bed, and spoke his next words cautiously in Turlington's ear.

'Another man in the way?'

'Yes.'

The giant shook his bald bestial head dolefully. 'Too late. I'm past the job. Look here.'

He held up his hand, and showed it trembling incessantly. 'I'm an old man,' he said, and let his hand drop heavily again on the bed beside him.

Turlington looked at the door, and whispered back –

'The man is as old as you are. And the money is worth having.'

'How much?'

'A hundred pounds.'

The eyes of Thomas Wildfang fastened greedily on Turlington's face. 'Let's hear,' he said. 'Softly, captain. Let's hear.'

* * * * * *

When the women came back with the clothes, Turlington had left the room. Their promised reward lay waiting for them on the table, and Thomas Wildfang was eager to dress himself and be gone. They could get but one answer from him to every question they put. He had business in hand, which was not to be delayed. They would see him again in a day or two, with money in his purse. With that assurance he took his cudgel from the corner of the room, and stalked out swiftly by the back door of the house into the night.

ELEVENTH SCENE

OUTSIDE THE HOUSE

The evening was chilly, but not cold for the time of year. There was no moon. The stars were out, and the wind was quiet. Upon the whole, the inhabitants of the little Somersetshire village of Baxdale agreed that it was as fine a Christmas Eve as they could remember for some years past.

Towards eight in the evening the one small street of the village was empty, except at that part of it which was occupied by the public-house. For the most part, people gathered round their firesides, with an eye to their suppers, and watched the process of cooking comfortably indoors. The old bare grey church, situated at some little distance from the village, looked a lonelier object than usual in the dim starlight. The vicarage, nestling close under the shadow of the church tower, threw no illumination of firelight or candlelight on the dreary scene.

The clergyman's shutters fitted well, and the clergyman's curtains were closely drawn. The one ray of light that cheered the wintry darkness streamed from the unguarded window of a lonely house, separated from the vicarage by the whole length of the churchyard. A man stood at the window, holding back the shutter, and looking out attentively over the dim void of the burial ground. The man was Richard Turlington. The room in which he was watching was a room in his own house.

A momentary spark of light flashed up, as from a kindled match, in the burial ground. Turlington instantly left the empty room in which he had been watching. Passing down the back garden of the house, and crossing a narrow lane at the bottom of it, he opened a gate in a low stone wall beyond, and entered the churchyard. The shadowy figure of a man of great stature, lurking among the graves, advanced to meet him. Midway in the dark and lonely place, the two stopped and consulted together in whispers. Turlington spoke first.

'Have you taken up your quarters at the public-house in the village?'

'Yes, master.'

'Did you find your way, while the daylight lasted, to the deserted malthouse behind my orchard wall?'

'Yes, master.'

'Now listen – we have no time to lose. Hide there, behind that monument. Before nine o'clock to-night you will see me cross the churchyard, as far as this place, with the man you are to wait for. He is going to spend an hour with the vicar, at the house yonder. I shall stop short here, and say to him, "You can't miss your way in the dark now – I will go back." When I am far enough away from him, I shall blow a call on my whistle. The moment you hear the call, follow the man, and drop him before he gets out of the churchyard. Have you got your cudgel?'

Thomas Wildfang held up his cudgel. Turlington took him by the arm, and felt it suspiciously.

'You have had an attack of the horrors, already,' he said. 'What does this trembling mean?'

He took a spirit-flask from his pocket as he spoke. Thomas Wildfang snatched it out of his hand, and emptied it at a draught. 'All right now, master,' he said. Turlington felt his arm once more. It was steadier already. Wildfang brandished his cudgel, and struck a heavy blow with it on one of the turf-mounds near them. 'Will that drop him, captain?' he asked. Turlington went on with his instructions.

'Rob him when you have dropped him. Take his money and his jewellery. I want to have the killing of him attributed to robbery as the motive. Make sure before you leave him that he is dead. Then go to the malthouse. There is no fear of your being seen; all the people will be indoors, keeping Christmas Eve. You will find a change of clothes hidden in the malthouse, and an old cauldron full of quicklime. Destroy the clothes you have got on, and dress yourself in the other clothes that you find. Follow the cross-road, and when it brings you into the high road, turn to the left; a four-mile walk will take you to the town of Harminster. Sleep there to-night, and travel to London by the train in the morning. The next day go to my office, see the head clerk, and say, "I have come to sign my receipt." Sign it in your own name, and you will receive your hundred pounds. There are your instructions. Do you understand them?'

Wildfang nodded his head in silent token that he understood, and disappeared again among the graves. Turlington went back to the house.

He had advanced midway across the garden, when he was startled by the sound of footsteps in the lane – at that part of it which skirted one of the corners of the house. Hastening forward, he placed himself behind a projection in the wall, so as to see the person pass across the stream of light from the uncovered window of the room that he had left. The stranger was walking rapidly. All Turlington could see, as he crossed the field of light, was that his hat was pulled over his eyes, and that he had a thick beard and moustachio. Describing the man to the servant on entering the house, he was informed that a stranger with a large beard had been seen about the neighbourhood for some days past. The account he had given of himself stated that he was a surveyor, engaged in taking measurements for a new map of that part of the country, shortly to be published.

The guilty mind of Turlington was far from feeling satisfied with the meagre description of the stranger thus rendered. He could not be engaged in surveying in the dark. What could he want in the desolate neighbourhood of the house and churchyard at that time of night?

The man wanted – what the man found a little lower down the lane, hidden in a dismantled part of the churchyard wall – a letter from a young lady. Read by the light of the pocket lantern which he carried with him, the letter first congratulated this person on the complete success of his disguise – and then promised that the writer would be ready at her bedroom window for flight the next morning, before the house was astir. The signature was 'Natalie,' and the person addressed was 'Dearest Launce.'

In the mean while, Turlington barred the window-shutters of the room, and looked at his watch. It wanted only a quarter to nine o'clock. He took his dog-whistle from the chimney-piece, and turned his steps at once in the direction of the drawing-room, in which his guests were passing the evening.

TWELFTH SCENE

INSIDE THE HOUSE

The scene in the drawing-room represented the ideal of domestic comfort. The fire of wood and coal mixed, burnt brightly; the lamps shed a soft glow of light; the solid shutters and the thick red curtains kept the cold night air on the outer side of two long windows, which opened on the back garden. Snug arm-chairs were placed in every part of the room. In one of them Sir Joseph reclined, fast asleep; in another, Miss Lavinia sat knitting; a third chair, apart from the rest, near a round table

in one corner of the room, was occupied by Natalie. Her head
was resting on her hand; an unread book lay open on her lap.
She looked pale and harassed; anxiety and suspense had worn
her down to the shadow of her former self. On entering the
room, Turlington purposely closed the door with a bang.
Natalie started. Miss Lavinia looked up reproachfully. The
object was achieved – Sir Joseph was roused from his sleep.

'If you are going to the vicar's to-night, Graybrooke,' said
Turlington, 'it's time you were off, isn't it?'

Sir Joseph rubbed his eyes, and looked at the clock on the
mantlepiece. 'Yes, yes, Richard,' he answered drowsily, 'I
suppose I must go. Where is my hat?'

His sister and his daughter both joined in trying to persuade
him to send an excuse instead of groping his way to the
vicarage in the dark. Sir Joseph hesitated as usual. He and the
vicar had run up a sudden friendship, on the strength of their
common enthusiasm for the old-fashioned game of
backgammon. Victorious over his opponent on previous
evening at Turlington's house, Sir Joseph had promised to pass
that evening at the vicarage, and give the vicar his revenge.
Observing his indecision, Turlington cunningly irritated him by
affecting to believe that he was really unwilling to venture out
in the dark. 'I'll see you safe across the churchyard,' he said;
'and the vicar's servant will see you safe back.' The tone in
which he spoke instantly roused Sir Joseph. 'I am not in my
second childhood yet, Richard,' he replied, testily. 'I can find
my way by myself.' He kissed his daughter on the forehead.
'No fear, Natalie. I shall be back in time for the mulled claret.
No, Richard, I won't trouble you.' He kissed his hand to his
sister and went out into the hall for his hat; Turlington
following him with a rough apology, and asking as a favour to
be permitted to accompany him part of the way only. The
ladies, left behind in the drawing-room, heard the apology
accepted by kind-hearted Sir Joseph. The two went out
together.

'Have you noticed Richard since his return?' asked Miss
Lavinia. 'I fancy he must have heard bad news in London. He
looks as if he had something on his mind.'

'I haven't remarked it, aunt.'

For the time, no more was said. Miss Lavinia went monotonously on with her knitting. Natalie pursued her own anxious thoughts over the unread pages of the book in her lap. Suddenly the deep silence out of doors and in was broken by a shrill whistle, sounding from the direction of the churchyard. Natalie started with a faint cry of alarm. Miss Lavinia looked up from her knitting.

'My dear child! your nerves must be sadly out of order. What is there to be frightened at?'

'I'm not very well, aunt. It is so still here at night, the slightest noises startle me.'

There was another interval of silence. It was past nine o'clock when they heard the back door opened and closed again. Turlington came hurriedly into the drawing-room, as if he had some reason for wishing to rejoin the ladies as soon as possible. To the surprise of both of them, he sat down abruptly in a corner, with his face to the wall, and took up the newspaper, without casting a look at them or uttering a word.

'Is Joseph safe at the vicarage?' asked Miss Lavinia.

'All right.' He gave the answer in a short, surly tone, still without looking round.

Miss Lavinia tried him again. 'Did you hear a whistle while you were out? It quite startled Natalie in the stillness of this place.'

He turned half way round. 'My shepherd, I suppose,' he said, after a pause – 'whistling for his dog.' He turned back again and immersed himself in his newspaper.

Miss Lavinia beckoned to her niece and pointed significantly to Turlington. After one reluctant look at him, Natalie laid her head wearily on her aunt's shoulder. 'Sleepy, my dear?' whispered the old lady. 'Uneasy, aunt – I don't know why,' Natalie whispered back. 'I would give the world to be in London, and to hear the carriages going by, and the people talking in the street.'

Turlington suddenly dropped his newspaper. 'What's the secret between you two?' he called out roughly. 'What are you whispering about?'

'We wish not to disturb you over your reading, that is all,' said Miss Lavinia, coldly. 'Has anything happened to vex you, Richard?'

'What the devil makes you think that?'

The old lady was offended, and showed it by saying nothing more. Natalie nestled closer to her aunt. One after another the clock ticked off the minutes with painful distinctness in the stillness of the room. Turlington suddenly threw aside the newspaper and left his corner. 'Let's be good friends!' he burst out, with a clumsy assumption of gaiety. 'This isn't keeping Christmas Eve. Let's talk and be sociable. Dearest Natalie!' He threw his arm roughly round Natalie, and drew her by main force away from her aunt. She turned deadly pale, and struggled to release herself. 'I am suffering – I am ill – let me go!' He was deaf to her entreaties. 'What! your husband that is to be, treated in this way? Mustn't I have a kiss? – I will!' He held her closer with one hand, and, seizing her head with the other, tried to turn her lips to him. She resisted with the inbred nervous strength which the weakest woman living has in reserve when she is outraged. Half indignant, half terrified, at Turlington's roughness, Miss Lavinia rose to interfere. In a moment more he would have had two women to overpower instead of one, when a noise outside the window suddenly suspended the ignoble struggle.

There was a sound of footsteps on the gravel walk which ran between the house-wall and the garden-lawn. It was followed by a tap – a single, faint tap, no more – on one of the panes of glass.

They all three stood still. For a moment more, nothing was audible. Then there was a heavy shock, as of something falling outside. Then a groan, then another interval of silence – a long silence, interrupted no more.

Turlington's arm dropped from Natalie. She drew back to her aunt. Looking at him instinctively, in the natural expectation that he would take the lead in penetrating the mystery of what had happened outside the window, the two women were thunderstruck to see that he was, to all appearance, even more startled and more helpless than they were. 'Richard,' said Miss Lavinia, pointing to the window, 'there is something wrong out there. See what it is.' He stood motionless, as if he had not heard her, his eyes fixed on the window, his face livid with terror.

The silence outside was broken once more; this time by a call for help.

A cry of horror burst from Natalie. The voice outside – rising wildly, then suddenly dying away again – was not entirely strange to *her* ears. She tore aside the curtain. With voice and hand she roused her aunt to help her. The two lifted the heavy bar from its socket; they opened the shutters and the window. The cheerful light of the room flowed out over the body of a prostrate man, lying on his face. They turned the man over. Natalie lifted his head.

Her father!

His face was bedabbled with blood. A wound, a frightful wound, was visible on the side of his bare head, high above the ear. He looked at her; his eyes recognized her, before he fainted again in her arms. His hands and his clothes were covered with earth stains. He must have traversed some distance: in that dreadful condition he must have faltered and fallen more than once before he reached the house. His sister wiped the blood from his face. His daughter called on him frantically to forgive her before he died – the harmless, gentle, kind-hearted father, who had never said a hard word to her! The father whom she had deceived!

The terrified servants hurried into the room. Their appearance roused their master from the extraordinary stupor that had seized him. He was at the window before the footman could get there. The two lifted Sir Joseph into the room, and laid him on the sofa. Natalie knelt by him, supporting his head. Miss Lavinia staunched the flowing blood with her handkerchief. The women-servants brought linen and cold water. The man hurried away for the doctor, who lived on the other side of the village. Left alone again with Turlington, Natalie noticed that his eyes were fixed in immovable scrutiny on her father's head. He never said a word. He looked, looked, looked at the wound.

The doctor arrived. Before either the daughter or the sister of the injured man could put the question, Turlington put it – 'Will he live or die?'

The doctor's careful finger probed the wound.

'Make your minds easy. A little lower down, or in front, the blow might have been serious. As it is, there is no harm done. Keep him quiet and he will be all right again in two or three days.'

Hearing those welcome words, Natalie and her aunt sank on their knees in silent gratitude. After dressing the wound, the doctor looked round for the master of the house. Turlington, who had been so breathlessly eager but a few minutes since, seemed to have lost all interest in the case now. He stood apart, at the window, looking out towards the churchyard, thinking. The questions which it was the doctor's duty to ask, were answered by the ladies. The servants assisted in examining the injured man's clothes: they discovered that his watch and purse were both missing. When it became necessary to carry him upstairs, it was the footman who assisted the doctor. The footman's master, without a word of explanation, walked out bare-headed into the back garden, on the search, as the doctor and the servants supposed, for some trace of the robber who had attempted Sir Joseph's life.

His absence was hardly noticed at the time. The difficulty of conveying the wounded man to his room, absorbed the attention of all the persons present.

Sir Joseph partially recovered his senses while they were taking him up the steep and narrow stairs. Carefully as they carried the patient, the motion wrung a groan from him before they reached the top. The bedroom corridor, in the rambling irregularly built house, rose and fell on different levels. At the door of the first bed-chamber the doctor asked a little anxiously if that was the room. No; there were three more stairs to go down, and a corner to turn, before they could reach it. The first room was Natalie's. She instantly offered it for her father's use. The doctor (seeing that it was the airiest as well as the nearest room) accepted the proposal. Sir Joseph had been laid comfortably in his daughter's bed; the doctor had just left them, with renewed assurances that they need feel no anxiety – when they heard a heavy step below stairs. Turlington had re-entered the house.

(He had been looking, as they had supposed, for the ruffian who had attacked Sir Joseph; with a motive, however, for the search, at which it was impossible for other persons to guess. His own safety was now bound up in the safety of Thomas Wildfang. As soon as he was out of sight in the darkness, he made straight for the malthouse. The change of clothes was there untouched; not a trace of his accomplice was to be seen. Where else to look for him it was impossible to tell. Turlington had no alternative but to go back to the house, and ascertain if suspicion had been aroused in his absence.)

He had only to ascend the stairs, and to see, through the open door, that Sir Joseph had been placed in his daughter's room.

'What does this mean?' he asked roughly.

Before it was possible to answer him the footman appeared with a message. The doctor had come back to the door to say that he would take on himself the necessary duty of informing the constable of what had happened, on his return to the village. Turlington started and changed colour. If Wildfang was found by others, and questioned in his employer's absence, serious consequences might follow. 'The constable is my business,' said Turlington, hurriedly descending the stairs; 'I'll go with the doctor.' They heard him open the door below, then close it again (as if some sudden thought had struck him) and call to the footman. The house was badly provided with servants' bed-rooms. The women-servants only slept indoors. The footman occupied a room over the stables. Natalie and her aunt heard Turlington dismiss the man for the night, an hour earlier than usual at least. His next proceeding was stranger still. Looking cautiously over the stairs, Natalie saw him lock all the doors on the ground floor and take out the keys. When he went away she heard him lock the front door behind him. Incredible as it seemed, there could be no doubt of the fact – the inmates of the house were imprisoned till he came back. What did it mean?

(It meant that Turlington's vengeance still remained to be wreaked on the woman who had deceived him. It meant that

Sir Joseph's life still stood between the man who had compassed his death and the money which the man was resolved to have. It meant that Richard Turlington was driven to bay, and that the horror and the peril of the night were not at an end yet.)

Natalie and her aunt looked at each other across the bed on which Sir Joseph lay. He had fallen into a kind of doze; no enlightenment could come to them from *him*. They could only ask each other, with beating hearts and baffled minds, what Richard's conduct meant – they could only feel instinctively that some dreadful discovery was hanging over them. The aunt was the calmer of the two – there was no secret weighing heavily on *her* conscience. *She* could feel the consolations of religion. 'Our dear one is spared to us, my love,' said the old lady gently. 'God has been good to us. We are in His hands. If we know that, we know enough.'

As she spoke there was a loud ring at the door bell. The women-servants crowded into the bedroom in alarm. Strong in numbers, and encouraged by Natalie – who roused herself and led the way – they confronted the risk of opening the window and of venturing out on the balcony which extended along that side of the house. A man was dimly visible below. He called to them in thick unsteady accents. The servants recognized him: he was the telegraphic messenger from the railway. They went down to speak to him – and returned with a telegram which had been pushed in under the door. The distance from the station was considerable; the messenger had been 'Keeping Christmas' in more than one beershop on his way to the house; and the delivery of the telegram had been delayed for some hours. It was addressed to Natalie. She opened it – looked at it – dropped it – and stood speechless; her lips parted in horror, her eyes staring vacantly straight before her.

Miss Lavinia took the telegram from the floor, and read these lines:–

'Lady Winwood, Hertford Street, London. To Natalie Graybrooke, Church Meadows, Baxdale, Somersetshire. Dreadful news. R.T. has discovered your marriage to Launce. The truth has been kept from me till to-day (24th). Instant flight with your husband is your only chance. I would have communicated with Launce, but I do not know his address. You will receive this, I hope and believe, before R.T. can return to Somersetshire. Telegraph back, I entreat you, to say that you are safe. I shall follow my message if I do not hear from you in reasonable time.'

Miss Lavinia lifted her grey head, and looked at her niece. 'Is this true?' she said – and pointed to the venerable face laid back, white, on the white pillow of the bed. Natalie sank forward as her eyes met the eyes of her aunt. Miss Lavinia saved her from falling insensible on the floor.

* * * * * *

The confession had been made. The words of penitence and the words of pardon had been spoken. The peaceful face of the father still lay hushed in rest. One by one, the minutes succeeded each other uneventfully in the deep tranquillity of the night. It was almost a relief when the silence was disturbed once more by another sound outside the house. A pebble was thrown up at the window, and a voice called out cautiously. 'Miss Lavinia!'

They recognized the voice of the man-servant, and at once opened the window.

He had something to say to the ladies in private. How could he say it? A domestic circumstance which had been marked by Launce, as favourable to the contemplated elopement, was now noticed by the servant as lending itself readily to effecting the necessary communication with the ladies. The lock of the gardener's tool-house (in the shrubbery close by) was under repair; and the gardener's ladder was accessible to any one who wanted it. At the short height of the balcony from the ground, the ladder was more than long enough for the purpose required. In a few minutes the servant had mounted to the balcony, and could speak to Natalie and her aunt at the window.

'I can't rest quiet,' said the man. 'I'm off on the sly to see what's going on down in the village. It's hard on ladies like you to be locked in here. Is there anything I can do for either of you?'

Natalie took up Lady Winwood's telegram. 'Launce ought to see this,' she said to her aunt. 'He will be here at daybreak,' she added, in a whisper, 'if I don't tell him what has happened.'

Miss Lavinia turned pale. 'If he and Richard meet——!' she began. 'Tell him!' she added hurriedly – 'tell him before it is too late!'

Natalie wrote a few lines (addressed to Launce in his assumed name at his lodgings in the village) enclosing Lady Winwood's telegram, and entreating him to do nothing rash. When the servant had disappeared with the letter, there was one hope in her mind and in her aunt's mind, which each was ashamed to acknowledge to the other – the hope that Launce would face the very danger that they dreaded for him, and come to the house.

They had not been long alone again, when Sir Joseph drowsily opened his eyes and asked what they were doing in his room. They told him gently that he was ill. He put his hand up to his head, and said they were right; and so dropped off again into slumber. Worn out by the emotions through which they had passed, the two women silently waited for the march of events. The same stupor of resignation possessed them both. They had secured the door and the window. They had prayed together. They had kissed the quiet face on the pillow. They had said to each other, 'We will live with him or die with him as God pleases.' Miss Lavinia sat by the bedside. Natalie was on a stool at her feet – with her eyes closed, and her head on her aunt's knee.

Time went on. The clock in the hall had struck – ten or eleven, they were not sure which – when they heard the signal which warned them of the servant's return from the village. He brought news, and more than news, he brought a letter from Launce.

Natalie read these lines:–

'I shall be with you, dearest, almost as soon as you receive this. The bearer will tell you what has happened in the village – your note throws a new light on it all. I only remain behind to go to the vicar (who is also the magistrate here), and declare myself your husband. All disguise must be at an end now. My place is with you and yours. It is even worse than your worst fears. Turlington was at the bottom of the attack on your father.

Judge if you have not need of your husband's protection after that! – L.'

Natalie handed the letter to her aunt, and pointed to the sentence which asserted Turlington's guilty knowledge of the attempt on Sir Joseph's life. In silent horror the two women looked at each other, recalling what had happened earlier in the evening, and understanding it now. The servant roused them to a sense of present things, by entering on the narrative of his discoveries in the village.

The place was all astir when he reached it. An old man – a stranger in Baxdale – had been found lying in the road, close to the church, in a fit; and the person who had discovered him had been no other than Launce himself. He had, literally, stumbled over the body of Thomas Wildfang in the dark, on his way back to his lodgings in the village.

'The gentleman gave the alarm, Miss,' said the servant, describing the event, as it had been related to him, 'and the man – a huge big old man – was carried to the inn. The landlord identified him; he had taken lodgings at the inn that day, and the constable found valuable property on him – a purse of money and a gold watch and chain. There was nothing to show who the money and the watch belonged to. It was only when my master and the doctor got to the inn that it was known whom he had robbed and tried to murder. All he let out in his wanderings before they came, was that some person had set him on to do it. He called the person "Captain," and sometimes "Captain Goward." It was thought – if you could trust the ravings of a madman – that the fit took him while he was putting his hand on Sir Joseph's heart to feel if it had stopped beating. A sort of a vision (as I understand it) must have overpowered him at the moment. They tell me he raved about the sea bursting into the churchyard, and a drowning sailor floating by on a hen-coop; a sailor who dragged him down to hell by the hair of his head, and such like horrible nonsense, Miss. He was still screeching, at the worst of the fit, when my master and the doctor came into the room. At sight of one or other of them – it is thought of Mr Turlington, seeing that he came first – he held his peace on a sudden, and then fell back in convulsions in the arms of the men who were holding him. The doctor gave it a learned name, signifying drink-madness, and said the case was hopeless. However, he ordered the room to be cleared of the crowd to see what he could do. My master was reported to be still with the doctor, waiting to see whether the man lived or died, when I left the village, Miss, with the gentleman's answer to your note. I didn't dare stay to hear how it ended, for fear of Mr Turlington's finding me out.'

Having reached the end of his narrative, the man looked round restlessly towards the window. It was impossible to say when his master might not return, and it might be as much as his life was worth to be caught in the house after he had been locked out of it. He begged permission to open the window, and make his escape back to the stables while there was still time. As he unbarred the shutter they were startled by a voice hailing them from below. It was Launce's voice, calling to Natalie. The servant disappeared – and Natalie was in Launce's arms before she could breathe again.

For one delicious moment she let her head lie on his breast: then she suddenly pushed him away from her. 'Why do you come here? He will kill you if he finds you in the house. Where is he?'

Launce knew even less of Turlington's movements than the servant. 'Wherever he is, thank God, I am here before him!' That was all the answer he could give.

Natalie and her aunt heard him in silent dismay. Sir Joseph woke and recognized Launce before a word more could be said. 'Ah, my dear boy!' he murmured faintly. 'It's pleasant to see you again. How do you come here?' He was quite satisfied with the first excuse that suggested itself. 'We'll talk about it to-morrow,' he said, and composed himself to rest again.

Natalie made a second attempt to persuade Launce to leave the house.

'We don't know what may have happened,' she said. 'He may have followed you on your way here. He may have purposely let you enter his house. Leave us while you have the chance.'

Miss Lavinia added her persuasions. They were useless. Launce quietly closed the heavy window-shutters, lined with iron, and put up the bar. Natalie wrung her hands in despair.

'Have you been to the magistrate?' she asked. 'Tell us, at least, are you here by his advice? Is he coming to help us?'

Launce hesitated. If he had told the truth, he must have acknowledged that he was there in direct opposition to the magistrate's advice. He answered evasively, 'If the vicar doesn't come, the doctor will. I have told him Sir Joseph must be moved. Cheer up, Natalie! The doctor will be here as soon as Turlington.'

As the name passed his lips – without a sound outside to prepare them for what was coming – the voice of Turlington himself suddenly penetrated into the room, speaking close behind the window, on the outer side.

'You have broken into my house in the night,' said the voice. 'And you don't escape *this* way.'

Miss Lavinia sank on her knees. Natalie flew to her father. His eyes were wide open in terror; he moaned, feebly recognizing the voice. The next sound that was heard was the sound made by the removal of the ladder from the balcony. Turlington, having descended by it, had taken it away. Natalie had but too accurately guessed what would happen. The death of the villain's accomplice had freed him from all apprehension in that quarter. He had deliberately dogged Launce's steps, and had deliberately allowed him to put himself in the wrong by effecting a secret entrance into the house.

There was an interval – a horrible interval – and then they heard the front door opened. Without stopping (judging by the absence of sound) to close it again, Turlington rapidly ascended the stairs and tried the locked door.

'Come out, and give yourself up!' he called through the door. 'I have got my revolver with me, and I have a right to fire on a man who has broken into my house. If the door isn't opened before I count three, your blood be on your own head. One!'

Launce was armed with nothing but his stick. He advanced, without an instant's hesitation, to give himself up. Natalie threw her arms round him and clasped him fast before he could reach the door.

'Two!' cried the voice outside, as Launce struggled to force her from him. At the same moment his eye turned towards the bed. It was exactly opposite the door – it was straight in the line of fire! Sir Joseph's life (as Turlington had deliberately calculated) was actually in greater danger than Launce's life. He tore himself free, rushed to the bed, and took the old man in his arms to lift him out.

'Three!'

The crash of the report sounded. The bullet came through the door, grazed Launce's left arm, and buried itself in the pillow, at the very place on which Sir Joseph's head had rested the moment before. Launce had saved his father-in-law's life. Turlington had fired his first shot for the money, and had not got it yet.

They were safe in the corner of the room, on the same side as the door – Sir Joseph, helpless as a child, in Launce's arms; the women pale, but admirably calm. They were safe for the moment, when the second bullet (fired at an angle) tore its way through the wall on their right hand.

'I hear you,' cried the voice of the miscreant on the other side of the door. 'I'll have you yet – through the wall.'

There was a pause. They heard his hand sounding the wall, to find out where there was solid wood in the material of which it was built, and where there was plaster only. At that dreadful moment Launce's composure never left him. He laid Sir Joseph softly on the floor, and signed to Natalie and her aunt to lie down by him in silence. Their lives depended now on neither their voices nor their movements telling the murderer where to fire. He chose his place. The barrel of the revolver grated as he laid it against the wall. He touched the hair-trigger. A faint *click* was the only sound that followed. The third barrel had missed fire.

They heard him ask himself, with an oath, 'What's wrong with it now?'

There was a pause of silence.

Was he examining the weapon?

Before they could ask themselves the question, the report of the exploding charge burst on their ears. It was instantly followed by a heavy fall. They looked at the opposite wall of the room. No sign of a bullet there or anywhere.

Launce signed to them not to move yet. They waited, and listened. Nothing stirred on the landing outside.

Suddenly there was a disturbance of the silence in the lower regions — a clamour of many voices at the open house door. Had the firing of the revolver been heard at the vicarage? Yes! They recognized the vicar's voice among the others. A moment more, and they heard a general exclamation of horror on the stairs. Launce opened the door of the room. He instantly closed it again before Natalie could follow him.

The dead body of Turlington lay on the landing outside. The charge in the fourth barrel of the revolver had exploded while he was looking at it. The bullet had entered his mouth and killed him on the spot.

DOCUMENTARY HINTS, IN CONCLUSION

FIRST HINT

(*Derived from Lady Winwood's Card-Rack.*)

'Sir Joseph Graybrooke and Miss Graybrooke request the honour of Lord and Lady Winwood's company to dinner, on Wednesday, February 10, at half-past seven o'clock. To meet Mr and Mrs Launcelot Linzie on their return.'

SECOND HINT

(*Derived from a recent money article in a morning newspaper.*)

'We are requested to give the fullest contradiction to unfavourable rumours lately in circulation respecting the firm of Pizzituti, Turlington, and Branca. Some temporary derangement in the machinery of the business was undoubtedly produced in consequence of the sudden death of the lamented managing partner, Mr Turlington, by the accidental discharge of a revolver which he was examining. Whatever temporary obstacles may have existed are now overcome. We are informed, on good authority, that the well-known house of Messrs Bulpit Brothers has an interest in the business, and will carry it on until further notice.'

TWO SEA-STORIES

'BLOW UP WITH THE BRIG!'

A SAILOR'S STORY

I have got an alarming confession to make. I am haunted by a Ghost.

If you were to guess for a hundred years, you would never guess what my ghost is. I shall make you laugh to begin with – and afterwards I shall make your flesh creep. My Ghost is the ghost of a Bedroom Candlestick.

Yes, a bedroom candlestick and candle or a flat candlestick and candle – put it which way you like – that is what haunts me. I wish it was something pleasanter and more out of the common way; a beautiful lady, or a mine of gold and silver, or a cellar of wine and a coach and horses, and such-like. But, being what it is, I must take it for what it is, and make the best of it – and I shall thank you kindly if you will help me out by doing the same.

I am not a scholar myself; but I make bold to believe that the haunting of any man with anything under the sun, begins with the frightening of him. At any rate, the haunting of me with a bedroom candlestick and candle began with the frightening of me with a bedroom candlestick and candle – the frightening of me half out of my life; and, for the time being, the frightening of me altogether out of my wits. That is not a very pleasant thing to confess, before stating the particulars; but perhaps you will be the readier to believe that I am not a downright coward, because you find me bold enough to make a clean breast of it already, to my own great disadvantage, so far.

Here are the particulars, as well as I can put them:–

I was apprenticed to the sea when I was about as tall as my own walking-stick; and I made good enough use of my time to be fit for a mate's berth at the age of twenty-five years.

It was in the year eighteen hundred and eighteen, or nineteen, I am not quite certain which, that I reached the before-mentioned age of twenty-five. You will please to excuse my memory not being very good for dates, names, numbers, places, and such-like. No fear, though, about the particulars I have undertaken to tell you of; I have got them all ship-shape in my recollection; I can see them, at this moment, as clear as noonday in my own mind. But there is a mist over what went before, and, for the matter of that, a mist likewise over much that came after – and it's not very likely to lift at my time of life, is it?

Well, in eighteen hundred and eighteen, or nineteen, when there was peace in our part of the world – and not before it was wanted, you will say – there was fighting, of a certain scampering, scrambling kind, going on in that old battle-field, which we seafaring men know by the name of the Spanish Main.

The possessions that belonged to the Spaniards in South America had broken into open mutiny and declared for themselves years before. There was plenty of bloodshed between the new government and the old; but the new had got the best of it, for the most part, under one General Bolivar – a famous man in his time, though he seems to have dropped out of people's memories now. Englishmen and Irishmen with a turn for fighting, and nothing particular to do at home, joined the general as volunteers; and some of our merchants here found it a good venture to send supplies across the ocean to the popular side. There was risk enough, of course, in doing this; but where one speculation of the kind succeeded, it made up for two, at the least, that failed. And that's the true principle of trade, wherever I have met with it, all the world over.

Among the Englishmen who were concerned in this Spanish-American business, I, your humble servant, happened in a small way to be one.

I was then mate of a brig belonging to a certain firm in the City, which drove a sort of general trade, mostly in queer out-of-the-way places, as far from home as possible; and which freighted the brig, in the year I am speaking of, with a cargo of gunpowder for General Bolivar and his volunteers. Nobody knew anything about our instructions, when we sailed, except the captain; and he didn't half seem to like them. I can't rightly say how many barrels of powder we had on board, or how much each barrel held – I only know we had no other cargo. The name of the brig was the Good Intent – a queer name enough, you will tell me, for a vessel laden with gunpowder, and sent to help a revolution. And as far as this particular voyage was concerned, so it was. I mean that for a joke, and I hope you will encourage me by laughing at it.

The Good Intent was the craziest old tub of a vessel I ever went to sea in, and the worst found in all respects. She was two hundred and thirty, or two hundred and eighty tons burden, I forget which; and she had a crew of eight, all told – nothing like as many as we ought by rights to have had to work the brig. However, we were well and honestly paid our wages; and we had to set that against the chance of foundering at sea, and, on this occasion, likewise, the chance of being blown up into the bargain.

In consideration of the nature of our cargo, we were harassed with new regulations which we didn't at all like, relative to smoking our pipes and lighting our lanterns; and, as usual in such cases, the captain who made the regulations, preached what he didn't practise. Not a man of us was allowed to have a bit of lighted candle in his hand when he went below – except the skipper; and he used his light, when he turned in, or when he looked over his charts on the cabin table, just as usual.

This light was a common kitchen candle or 'dip,' and it stood in an old battered flat candlestick, with all the japan worn and melted off, and all the tin showing through. It would have been more seamanlike and suitable in every respect if he had had a lamp or lantern; but he stuck to his old candlestick; and that same old candlestick has ever afterwards stuck to *me*. That's another joke, if you please, and a better one than the first, in my opinion.

Well (I said 'well' before, but it's a word that helps a man on like), we sailed in the brig, and shaped our course, first, for the Virgin Islands, in the West Indies; and, after sighting them, we made for the Leeward Islands next; and then stood on due south, till the look-out at the mast-head hailed the deck, and said he saw land. That land was the coast of South America. We had had a wonderful voyage so far. We had lost none of our spars or sails, and not a man of us had been harassed to death at the pumps. It wasn't often the Good Intent made such a voyage as that, I can tell you.

I was sent aloft to make sure about the land, and I did make sure of it.

When I reported the same to the skipper, he went below, and had a look at his letter of instructions and the chart. When he came on deck again, he altered our course a trifle to the eastward – I forget the point on the compass, but that don't matter. What I do remember is, that it was dark before we closed in with the land. We kept the lead going, and hove the brig to in from four to five fathoms water, or it might be six – I can't say for certain. I kept a sharp eye to the drift of the vessel, none of us knowing how the currents ran on that coast. We all wondered why the skipper didn't anchor; but he said, No, he must first show a light at the foretop mast-head, and wait for an answering light on shore. We did wait, and nothing of the sort appeared. It was starlight and calm. What little wind there was came in puffs off the land. I suppose we waited, drifting a little to the westward, as I made it out, best part of an hour before anything happened – and then, instead of seeing the light on shore, we saw a boat coming towards us, rowed by two men only.

We hailed them, and they answered 'Friends!' and hailed us by our name. They came on board. One of them was an Irishman, and the other was a coffee-coloured native pilot, who jabbered a little English.

The Irishman handed a note to our skipper, who showed it to me. It informed us that the part of the coast we were off was not over safe for discharging our cargo, seeing that spies of the enemy (that is to say, of the old government) had been taken and shot in the neighbourhood the day before. We might trust the brig to the native pilot; and he had his instructions to take us to another part of the coast. The note was signed by the proper parties; so we let the Irishman go back alone in the boat, and allowed the pilot to exercise his lawful authority over the brig. He kept us stretching off from the land till noon the next day – his instructions, seemingly, ordering him to keep us well out of sight of the shore. We only altered our course, in the afternoon, so as to close in with the land again a little before midnight.

This same pilot was about as ill-looking a vagabond as ever I saw; a skinny, cowardly, quarrelsome mongrel, who swore at the men, in the vilest broken English, till they were every one of them ready to pitch him overboard. The skipper kept them quiet, and I kept them quiet, for the pilot being given us by our instructions, we were bound to make the best of him. Near nightfall, however, with the best will in the world to avoid it, I was unlucky enough to quarrel with him.

He wanted to go below with his pipe, and I stopped him, of course, because it was contrary to orders. Upon that, he tried to hustle by me, and I put him away with my hand. I never meant to push him down; but, somehow, I did. He picked himself up as quick as lightning, and pulled out his knife. I snatched it out of his hand, slapped his murderous face for him, and threw his weapon overboard. He gave me one ugly look, and walked aft. I didn't think much of the look then; but I remembered it a little too well afterwards.

We were close in with the land again, just as the wind failed us, between eleven and twelve that night; and dropped our anchor by the pilot's directions.

It was pitch dark, and a dead airless calm. The skipper was on deck with two of our best men for watch. The rest were below, except the pilot, who coiled himself up, more like a snake than a man, on the forecastle. It was not my watch till four in the morning. But I didn't like the look of the night, or the pilot, or the state of things generally, and I shook myself down on deck to get my nap there, and be ready for anything at a moment's notice. The last I remember was the skipper whispering to me that he didn't like the look of things either, and that he would go below and consult his instructions again. That is the last I remember, before the slow, heavy, regular roll of the old brig on the ground swell rocked me off to sleep.

I was awoke by a scuffle on the forecastle, and a gag in my mouth. There was a man on my breast, and a man on my legs; and I was bound hand and foot in half a minute.

The brig was in the hands of the Spaniards. They were swarming all over her. I heard six heavy splashes in the water, one after another. I saw the captain stabbed to the heart as he came running up the companion – and I heard a seventh splash in the water. Except myself, every soul of us on board had been murdered and thrown into the sea. Why I was left, I couldn't think, till I saw the pilot stoop over me with a lantern, and look, to make sure of who I was. There was a devilish grin on his face, and he nodded his head at me, as much as to say, *You* were the man who hustled me down and slapped my face, and I mean to play the game of cat and mouse with you in return for it!

I could neither move nor speak; but I could see the Spaniards take off the main hatch and rig the purchases for getting up the cargo. A quarter of an hour afterwards, I heard the sweeps of a schooner, or other small vessel, in the water. The strange craft was laid alongside of us; and the Spaniards set to work to discharge our cargo into her. They all worked hard except the pilot; and he came, from time to time, with his lantern, to have another look at me, and to grin and nod always in the same devilish way. I am old enough now not to be ashamed of confessing the truth; and I don't mind acknowledging that the pilot frightened me.

The fright, and the bonds, and the gag, and the not being able to stir hand or foot, had pretty nigh worn me out, by the time the Spaniards gave over work. This was just as the dawn broke. They had shifted a good part of our cargo on board their vessel, but nothing like all of it; and they were sharp enough to be off with what they had got, before daylight.

I need hardly say that I had made up my mind, by this time, to the worst I could think of. The pilot, it was clear enough, was one of the spies of the enemy, who had wormed himself into the confidence of our consignees without being suspected. He, or more likely his employers, had got knowledge enough of us to suspect what our cargo was; we had been anchored for the night in the safest berth for them to surprise us in; and we had paid the penalty of having a small crew, and consequently an insufficient watch. All this was clear enough – but what did the pilot mean to do with *me*?

On the word of a man, it makes my flesh creep, now, only to tell you what he did with me.

After all the rest of them were out of the brig, except the pilot and two Spanish seamen, these last took me up, bound and gagged as I was, lowered me into the hold of the vessel, and laid me along on the floor; lashing me to it with ropes' ends, so that I could just turn from one side to the other, but could not roll myself fairly over, so as to change my place. They then left me. Both of them were the worse for liquor; but the devil of a pilot was sober – mind that! – as sober as I am at the present moment.

I lay in the dark for a little while, with my heart thumping as if it was going to jump out of me. I lay about five minutes or so, when the pilot came down into the hold, alone.

He had the captain's cursed flat candlestick and a carpenter's awl in one hand, and a long thin twist of cotton yarn, well oiled, in the other. He put the candlestick, with a new 'dip' candle lighted in it, down on the floor, about two feet from my face, and close against the side of the vessel. The light was feeble enough; but it was sufficient to show a dozen barrels of gunpowder or more, left all round me in the hold of the brig. I began to suspect what he was after, the moment I noticed the barrels. The horrors laid hold of me from head to foot; and the sweat poured off my face like water.

I saw him go, next, to one of the barrels of powder standing against the side of the vessel, in a line with the candle, and about three feet, or rather better, away from it. He bored a hole in the side of the barrel with his awl; and the horrid powder came trickling out, as black as hell, and dripped into the hollow of his hand, which he held to catch it. When he had got a good handful, he stopped up the hole by jamming one end of his oiled twist of cotton-yarn fast into it; and he then rubbed the powder into the whole length of the yarn, till he had blackened every hairsbreadth of it.

The next thing he did – as true as I sit here, as true as the heaven above us all – the next thing he did was to carry the free end of his long, lean, black, frightful slow-match to the lighted candle alongside my face. He tied it (the bloody-minded villain!) in several folds, round the tallow dip, around a third of the distance down, measuring from the flame of the wick to the lip of the candlestick. He did that; he looked to see that my lashings were all safe; and then he put his face down close to mine, and whispered in my ear, 'Blow up with the brig!'

He was on deck again the moment after; and he and the two others shoved the hatch on over me. At the farthest end from where I lay, they had not fitted it down quite true, and I saw a blink of daylight glimmering in when I looked in that direction. I heard the sweeps of the schooner fall into the water – splash! splash! fainter and fainter, as they swept the vessel out in the dead calm, to be ready for the wind in the offing. Fainter and fainter, splash! splash! for a quarter of an hour or more.

While those sounds were in my ears, my eyes were fixed on the candle.

It had been freshly lit – if left to itself it would burn for between six and seven hours. The slow-match was twisted round it about a third of the way down; and therefore the flame would be about two hours reaching it. There I lay, gagged, bound, lashed to the floor; seeing my own life burning down with the candle by my side – there I lay, alone on the sea, doomed to be blown to atoms, and to see that doom drawing on, nearer and nearer with every fresh second of time, through nigh on two hours to come; powerless to help myself and speechless to call for help to others. The wonder to me is that I didn't cheat the flame, the slow-match, and the powder, and die of the horror of my situation before my first half-hour was out in the hold of the brig.

I can't exactly say how long I kept the command of my senses after I had ceased to hear the splash of the schooner's sweeps in the water. I can trace back everything I did and everything I thought, up to a certain point; but, once past that, I get all abroad, and lose myself in my memory now, much as I lost myself in my own feelings at the time.

The moment the hatch was covered over me, I began, as every other man would have begun in my place, with a frantic effort to free my hands. In the mad panic I was in, I cut my flesh with the lashings as if they had been knife-blades; but I never stirred them. There was less chance still of freeing my legs, or of tearing myself from the fastenings that held me to the floor. I gave in, when I was all but suffocated for want of breath. The gag, you will please to remember, was a terrible enemy to me; I could only breathe freely through my nose – and that is but a poor vent when a man is straining his strength as far as ever it will go.

I gave in, and lay quiet, and got my breath again; my eyes glaring and straining at the candle all the time.

While I was staring at it, the notion struck me of trying to blow out the flame by pumping a long breath at it suddenly through my nostrils. It was too high above me, and too far away from me, to be reached in that fashion. I tried, and tried, and tried – and then I gave in again and lay quiet again; always with my eyes glaring at the candle, and the candle glaring at *me*. The splash of the schooner's sweeps was very faint by this time. I could only just hear them in the morning stillness. Splash! splash! – fainter and fainter – splash! splash!

Without exactly feeling my mind going, I began to feel it getting queer, as early as this. The snuff of the candle was growing taller and taller, and the length of tallow between the flame and the slow-match, which was the length of my life, was getting shorter and shorter. I calculated that I had rather less than an hour and a half to live.

An hour and a half! Was there a chance, in that time, of a boat pulling off to the brig from shore? Whether the land near which the vessel was anchored was in possession of our side, or in possession of the enemy's side, I made out that they must, sooner or later, send to hail the brig, merely because she was a stranger in those parts. The question for *me* was, how soon? The sun had not risen yet, as I could tell by looking through the chink in the hatch. There was no coast village near us, as we all knew, before the brig was seized, by seeing no lights on shore. There was no wind, as I could tell by listening, to bring any strange vessel near. If I had had six hours to live, there might have been a chance for me, reckoning from sunrise to noon. But with an hour and a half, which had dwindled to an hour and a quarter by this time – or, in other words, with the earliness of the morning, the uninhabited coast, and the dead calm all against me – there was not the ghost of a chance. As I felt that, I had another struggle – the last – with my bonds; and only cut myself the deeper for my pains.

I gave in once more, and lay quiet, and listened for the splash of the sweeps.

Gone! Not a sound could I hear but the blowing of a fish, now and then, on the surface of the sea, and the creak of the brig's crazy old spars, as she rolled gently from side to side with the little swell there was on the quiet water.

An hour and a quarter. The wick grew terribly, as the quarter slipped away; and the charred top of it began to thicken and spread out mushroom-shape. It would fall off soon. Would it fall off red-hot, and would the swing of the brig cant it over the side of the candle, and let it down on the slow-match? If it would, I had about ten minutes to live instead of an hour.

This discovery set my mind for a minute on a new tack altogether. I began to ponder with myself what sort of a death blowing-up might be. Painful? Well, it would be, surely, too sudden for that. Perhaps just one crash, inside me, or outside me, or both, and nothing more? Perhaps not even a crash; that and death and the scattering of this living body of mine into millions of fiery sparks, might all happen in the same instant? I couldn't make it out; I couldn't settle how it would be. The minute of calmness in my mind left it, before I had half done thinking; and I got all abroad again.

When I came back to my thoughts, or when they came back to me (I can't say which), the wick was awfully tall, the flame was burning with a smoke above it, the charred top was broad and red, and heavily spreading out to its fall.

My despair and horror at seeing it, took me in a new way, which was good and right, at any rate, for my poor soul. I tried to pray; in my own heart, you will understand, for the gag put all lip-praying out of my power. I tried, but the candle seemed to burn it up in me. I struggled hard to force my eyes from the slow, murdering flame, and to look up through the chink in the hatch at the blessed daylight. I tried once, tried twice; and gave it up. I tried next only to shut my eyes, and keep them shut – once – twice – and the second time I did it. 'God bless old mother, and sister Lizzie; God keep them both, and forgive *me*.' That was all I had time to say, in my own heart, before my eyes opened again, in spite of me, and the flame of the candle flew into them, flew all over me, and burnt up the rest of my thoughts in an instant.

I couldn't hear the fish blowing now; I couldn't hear the creak of the spars; I couldn't think; I couldn't feel the sweat of my own death agony on my face – I could only look at the heavy, charred top of the wick. It swelled, tottered, bent over to one side, dropped – red hot at the moment of its fall – black and harmless, even before the swing of the brig had canted it over into the bottom of the candlestick.

I caught myself laughing.

Yes! laughing at the safe fall of the bit of wick. But for the gag I should have screamed with laughing. As it was, I shook with it inside me – shook till the blood was in my head, and I was all but suffocated for want of breath. I had just sense enough left to feel that my own horrid laughter, at that awful moment, was a sign of my brain going at last. I had just sense enough left to make another struggle before my mind broke loose like a frightened horse, and ran away with me.

One comforting look at the blink of daylight through the hatch was what I tried for once more. The fight to force my eyes from the candle and to get that one look at the daylight, was the hardest I had had yet; and I lost the fight. The flame had hold of my eyes as fast as the lashings had hold of my hands. I couldn't look away from it. I couldn't even shut my eyes, when I tried that next, for the second time. There was the wick, growing tall once more. There was the space of unburnt candle between the light and the slow-match shortened to an inch or less.

How much life did that inch leave me? Three-quarters of an hour? Half an hour? Fifty minutes? Twenty minutes? Steady! an inch of tallow candle would burn longer than twenty minutes. An inch of tallow! the notion of a man's body and soul being kept together by an inch of tallow! Wonderful! Why, the greatest king that sits on a throne can't keep a man's body and soul together; and here's an inch of tallow that can do what the king can't! There's something to tell mother, when I get home, which will surprise her more than all the rest of my voyages put together. I laughed inwardly, again, at the thought of that; and shook and swelled and suffocated myself, till the light of the candle leaped in through my eyes, and licked up the laughter, and burnt it out of me, and made me all empty, and cold, and quiet once more.

Mother and Lizzie. I don't know when they came back; but they did come back — not, as it seemed to me, into my mind this time; but right down bodily before me, in the hold of the brig.

Yes: sure enough, there was Lizzie, just as light-hearted as usual, laughing at me. Laughing! Well, why not? Who is to blame Lizzie for thinking I'm lying on my back, drunk in the cellar, with the beer barrels all round me? Steady! she's crying now — spinning round and round in a fiery mist, wringing her hands, screeching out for help — fainter and fainter, like the splash of the schooner's sweeps. Gone! — burnt up in the fiery mist. Mist? fire? no: neither one nor the other. It's mother makes the light — mother knitting, with ten flaming points at the ends of her fingers and thumbs, and slow-matches hanging in bunches all round her face instead of her own grey hair. Mother in her old arm-chair, and the pilot's long skinny hands hanging over the back of the chair, dripping with gunpowder. No! no gunpowder, no chair, no mother — nothing but the pilot's face, shining red hot, like a sun, in the fiery mist; turning upside down in the fiery mist; running backwards and forward along the slow-match, in the fiery mist; spinning millions of miles in a minute, in the fiery mist — spinning itself smaller and smaller into one tiny point, and that point darting on a sudden straight into my head — and then, all fire and all mist — no hearing, no seeing, no thinking, no feeling — the brig, the sea, my own self, the whole world, all gone together!

After what I've just told you, I know nothing and remember nothing, till I woke up (as it seemed to me) in a comfortable bed, with two rough and ready men like myself sitting on each side of my pillow, and a gentleman standing watching me at the foot of the bed. It was about seven in the morning. My sleep (or what seemed like my sleep to me) had lasted better than eight months — I was among my own countrymen in the island of Trinidad — the men at each side of my pillow were my keepers, turn and turn about — and the gentleman standing at the foot of the bed was the doctor. What I said and did in those eight months, I never have known and never shall. I woke out of it, as if it had been one long sleep — that's all I know.

It was another two months or more before the doctor thought it safe to answer the questions I asked him.

The brig had been anchored, just as I had supposed, off a part of the coast which was lonely enough to make the Spaniards pretty sure of no interruption, so long as they managed their murderous work quietly under cover of night.

My life had not been saved from the shore, but from the sea. An American vessel, becalmed in the offing, had made out the brig as the sun rose; and the captain having his time on his hands in consequence of the calm, and seeing a vessel anchored where no vessel had any reason to be, had manned one of his boats and sent his mate with it, to look a little closer into the matter, and bring back a report of what he saw.

What he saw, when he and his men found the brig deserted and boarded her, was a gleam of candlelight through the chink in the hatchway. The flame was within about a thread's breadth of the slow-match, when he lowered himself into the hold; and if he had not had the sense and coolness to cut the match in two with his knife, before he touched the candle, he and his men might have been blown up along with the brig, as well as me. The match caught and turned into sputtering red fire, in the very act of putting the candle out; and if the communication with the powder barrel had not been cut off, the Lord only knows what might have happened.

What became of the Spanish schooner and the pilot I have never heard from that day to this.

As for the brig, the Yankees took her, as they took me, to Trinidad, and claimed their salvage, and got it, I hope, for their own sakes. I was landed just in the same state as when they rescued me from the brig, that is to say, clean out of my senses. But, please to remember it was a long time ago; and, take my word for it, I was discharged cured, as I have told you. Bless your hearts, I'm all right now, as you may see. I'm a little shaken by telling the story, as is only natural – a little shaken, my good friends, that's all.

THE FATAL CRADLE

OTHERWISE, THE HEARTRENDING STORY OF MR HEAVYSIDES

There has never yet been discovered a man with a grievance, who objected to mention it. I am no exception to this general human rule. I have got a grievance; and I don't object to mention it. Compose your spirits to hear a pathetic story, and kindly picture me in your own mind as a baby five minutes old.

Do I understand you to say that I am too big and too heavy to be pictured in anybody's mind as a baby? Perhaps I may be – but don't mention my weight again, if you please. My weight has been the grand misfortune of my life. It spoilt all my prospects (as you will presently hear) before I was two days old.

My story begins thirty-one years ago, at eleven o'clock in the forenoon; and starts with the great mistake of my first appearance in this world, at sea, on board the merchant ship Adventure, Captain Gillop, five hundred tons burden, coppered and carrying an experienced surgeon.

In presenting myself to you (which I am now about to do) at that eventful period of my life, when I was from five to ten minutes old; and in withdrawing myself again from your notice (so as not to trouble you with more than a short story), before the time when I cut my first tooth, I need not hesitate to admit that I speak on hearsay knowledge only. It is knowledge, however, that may be relied on, for all that. My information comes from Captain Gillop, commander of the Adventure (who sent it to me in the form of a letter); from Mr Jolly, experienced surgeon of the Adventure (who wrote it for me – most unfeelingly, as I think – in the shape of a humorous narrative); and from Mrs Drabble, stewardess of the Adventure (who told me by word of mouth). Those three persons were, in various degrees, spectators – I may say, astonished spectators – of the events which I have now to relate.

The Adventure, at the time I speak of, was bound out from London to Australia. I suppose you know, without my telling you, that thirty years ago was long before the time of the gold-finding and the famous clipper ships. Building in the new colony, and sheep-farming far up inland, were the two main employments of those days; and the passengers on board our vessel were consequently builders or sheep-farmers, almost to a man.

A ship of five hundred tons, well loaded with cargo, doesn't offer first-rate accommodation to a large number of passengers. Not that the gentlefolks in the cabin had any great reason to complain. There, the passage-money, which was a good round sum, kept them what you call select. One or two berths, in this part of the ship, were even empty and going a begging, in consequence of there being only four cabin passengers. These are their names and descriptions:

Mr Sims, a middle-aged man, going out on a building speculation. Mr Purling, a weakly young gentleman, sent on a long sea-voyage for the benefit of his health. And Mr and Mrs Smallchild, a young married couple with a little independence, which Mr Smallchild proposed to make a large one by sheep-farming.

This gentleman was reported to the captain, as being very good company when on shore. But the sea altered him to a certain extent. When Mr Smallchild was not sick, he was eating and drinking; and when he was not eating and drinking, he was fast asleep. He was perfectly patient and good-humoured, and wonderfully nimble at running into his cabin when the qualms took him on a sudden – but, as for his being good company, nobody heard him say ten words together all through the voyage. And no wonder. A man can't talk, in the qualms; a man can't talk, while he is eating and drinking; and a man can't talk, when he is asleep. And that was Mr Smallchild's life. As for Mrs Smallchild, she kept her cabin from first to last. But you will hear more of her presently.

These four cabin passengers, as I have already remarked, were well enough off for their accommodation. But the miserable people in the steerage – a poor place, at the best of times, on board the Adventure – were all huddled together, men and women and children, higgledy-piggledy, like sheep in a pen; except that they hadn't got the same quantity of fine fresh air to blow over them. They were artisans and farm-labourers, who couldn't make it out in the old country. I have no information either of their exact numbers or of their names. It doesn't matter: there was only one family among them which need be mentioned particularly – namely, the family of the Heavysides. To wit, Simon Heavysides, intelligent and well-educated, a carpenter by trade; Susan Heavysides, his wife; and seven little Heavysides, their unfortunate offspring. —— My father and mother and brothers and sisters, did I understand you to say? Don't be in a hurry! I recommend you to wait a little before you make quite sure of that circumstance.

Though I myself had not, perhaps – strictly speaking – come on board when the vessel left London, my ill-luck, as I firmly believe, had shipped in the Adventure to wait for me – and decided the nature of the voyage accordingly.

Never was such a miserable time known. Stormy weather came down on us from all points of the compass, with intervals of light baffling winds, or dead calms. By the time the Adventure had been three months out, Captain Gillop's naturally sweet temper began to get soured. I leave you to say whether it was likely to be much improved by a piece of news which reached him from the region of the cabin, on the morning of the ninety-first day. It had fallen to a dead calm again; and the ship was rolling about helpless with her head all round the compass, when Mr Jolly (from whose facetious narrative I repeat all conversations, exactly as they passed) came on deck to the captain, and addressed him in these words:

'I have got some news that will rather surprise you,' said Mr Jolly, smiling and rubbing his hands. (Although the experienced surgeon has not shown much sympathy for my troubles, I won't deny that his disposition was as good as his name. To this day, no amount of bad weather or hard work can upset Mr Jolly's temper.)

'If it's news of a fair wind coming,' grumbled the captain, 'that would surprise me, on board this ship, I can promise you!'

'It's not exactly a wind coming,' said Mr Jolly. 'It's another cabin passenger.'

The captain looked round at the empty sea, with the land thousands of miles away, and with not a ship in sight – turned sharply on the experienced surgeon – eyed him hard – changed colour suddenly – and asked what he meant.

'I mean there's a fifth cabin passenger coming on board,' persisted Mr Jolly, grinning from ear to ear – 'introduced by Mrs Smallchild – likely to join us, I should say, towards evening – size, nothing to speak of – sex, not known at present – manners and customs, probably squally.'

'Do you really mean it?' asked the captain, backing away, and turning paler and paler.

'Yes; I do,' answered Mr Jolly, nodding hard at him. 'Then I'll tell you what,' cried Captain Gillop, suddenly flying into a violent passion, 'I won't have it! the infernal weather has worried me out of my life and soul already – and I won't have it! Put it off, Jolly – tell her there isn't room enough for that sort of thing on board my vessel. What does she mean by taking us all in, in this way? Shameful! shameful!'

'No! no!' remonstrated Mr Jolly. 'Don't look at it in that light. It's her first child, poor thing. How should *she* know? Give her a little more experience, and I dare say——'

'Where's her husband?' broke in the captain, with a threatening look. 'I'll speak my mind to her husband, at any rate.'

Mr Jolly consulted his watch before he answered.

'Half-past eleven,' he said. 'Let me consider a little. It's Mr

Smallchild's regular time just now for squaring accounts with the sea. He'll have done in a quarter of an hour. In five minutes more, he'll be fast asleep. At one o'clock he'll eat a hearty lunch, and go to sleep again. At half-past two, he'll square accounts as before – and so on, till night. You'll make nothing of Mr Smallchild, captain. Extraordinary man – wastes tissue, and repairs it again perpetually, in the most astonishing manner. If we are another month at sea, I believe we shall bring him into port totally comatose. —— Hullo! What do *you* want?'

The steward's mate had approached the quarter deck while the doctor was speaking. Was it a curious coincidence? This man also was grinning from ear to ear, exactly like Mr Jolly.

'You're wanted in the steerage, sir,' said the steward's mate to the doctor. 'A woman taken bad, name of Heavysides.'

'Nonsense!' cried Mr Jolly. 'Ha! ha! ha! You don't mean—— Eh?'

'That's it, sir, sure enough,' said the steward's mate, in the most positive manner.

Captain Gillop looked all round him, in silent desperation; lost his sea-legs for the first time these twenty years; staggered back till he was brought up all standing by the side of his own vessel; dashed his fist on the bulwark, and found language to express himself in, at the same moment.

'This ship is bewitched,' said the captain, wildly. 'Stop!' he called out, recovering himself a little, as the doctor bustled away to the steerage. 'Stop! If it's true, Jolly, send her husband here aft to me. Damme, I'll have it out with one of the husbands!' said the captain, shaking his fist viciously at the empty air.

Ten minutes passed; and then there came staggering towards the captain, tottering this way and that with the rolling of the becalmed vessel, a long, lean, melancholy, light-haired man, with a Roman nose, a watery blue eye, and a complexion profusely spotted with large brown freckles. This was Simon Heavysides, the intelligent carpenter, with the wife and the family of seven small children on board.

'Oh! you're the man, are you?' said the captain.

The ship lurched heavily; and Simon Heavysides staggered away with a run to the opposite side of the deck, as if he preferred going straight overboard into the sea, to answering the captain's question.

'You're the man – are you?' repeated the captain, following him, seizing him by the collar, and pinning him up fiercely against the bulwark. 'It's your wife – is it? You infernal rascal! what do you mean by turning my ship into a Lying-In Hospital? You have committed an act of mutiny; or, if it isn't mutiny, it's next door to it. I've put a man in irons for less! I've more than half a mind to put *you* in irons! Hold up, you slippery lubber! What do you mean by bringing passengers I don't bargain for on board my vessel? What have you got to say for yourself, before I clap the irons on you?'

'Nothing, sir,' answered Simon Heavysides, accepting the captain's strong language without a word of protest. 'As for the punishment you mentioned just now, sir,' continued Simon, 'I wish to say – having seven children more than I know how to provide for, and an eighth coming to make things worse – I respectfully wish to say, sir, that my mind is in irons already: and I don't know as it will make much difference if you put my body in irons along with it.'

The captain mechanically let go of the carpenter's collar: the mild despair of the man melted him in spite of himself.

'Why did you come to sea? Why didn't you wait ashore till it was all over?' asked the captain, as sternly as he could.

'It's no use waiting, sir,' remarked Simon. 'In our line of life as soon as it's over, it begins again. There's no end to it that I can see,' said the miserable carpenter, after a moment's meek consideration – 'except the grave.'

'Who's talking about the grave?' cried Mr Jolly, coming up at that moment. 'It's births we've got to do with on board this vessel – not burials. Captain Gillop, this woman, Mrs Heavysides, can't be left in your crowded steerage, in her present condition. She must be moved off into one of the empty berths – and the sooner the better, I can tell you!'

The captain began to look savage again. A steerage passenger in one of his 'state-rooms' was a nautical anomaly subversive of all discipline. He eyed the carpenter once more, as if he was mentally measuring him for a set of irons.

'I'm very sorry, sir,' Simon remarked, politely – 'very sorry that any inadvertence of mine or Mrs Heavysides——'

'Take your long carcase and your long tongue forward!' thundered the captain. 'When talking will mend matters, I'll send for you again. Give your own orders, Jolly,' he went on, resignedly, as Simon staggered off. 'Turn the ship into a nursery as soon as you like!'

Five minutes later – so expeditious was Mr Jolly – Mrs Heavysides appeared horizontally on deck, shrouded in blankets, and supported by three men. When this interesting procession passed the captain, he shrank aside from it with as vivid an appearance of horror as if a wild bull was being carried by him instead of a British matron.

The sleeping berths below opened on either side out of the main cabin. On the left-hand side (looking towards the ship's bowsprit) was Mrs Smallchild. On the right-hand side, opposite to her, the doctor established Mrs Heavysides. A partition of canvas was next run up, entirely across the main cabin. The smaller of the two temporary rooms thus made, lay nearest the stairs leading on deck, and was left free to the public. The larger was kept sacred to the doctor and his mysteries. When an old clothes-basket, emptied, cleaned, and comfortably lined with blankets (to serve for a makeshift cradle), had been, in due course of time, carried into the inner cabin, and had been placed midway between the two sleeping-berths, so as to be easily producible when wanted, the outward and visible preparations of Mr Jolly were complete; the male passengers had all taken refuge on deck; and the doctor and the stewardess were left in undisturbed possession of the lower regions.

While it was still early in the afternoon, the weather changed for the better. For once in a way, the wind came from a fair quarter; and the Adventure bowled along pleasantly before it almost on an even keel. Captain Gillop mixed with the little group of male passengers on the quarter-deck, restored to his sweetest temper; and set them his customary example, after dinner, of smoking a cigar.

'If this fine weather lasts, gentlemen,' he said, 'we shall make out very well with our meals up here; and we shall have our two small extra cabin passengers christened on dry land in a week's time, if their mothers approve of it. How do you feel in your mind, sir, about your good lady?'

Mr Smallchild (to whom the inquiry was addressed) had his points of external personal resemblance to Simon Heavysides. He was neither so tall nor so lean certainly – but he, too, had a Roman nose, and light hair, and watery blue eyes. With careful reference to his peculiar habits at sea, he had been placed conveniently close to the bulwark, and had been raised on a heap of old sails and cushions, so that he could easily get his head over the ship's side when occasion required. The food and drink which assisted in 'restoring his tissue,' when he was not asleep and not 'squaring accounts with the sea,' lay close to his hand. It was then a little after three o'clock; and the snore with which Mr Smallchild answered the captain's inquiry showed that he had got round again, with the regularity of clockwork, to the period of the day when he recruited himself with sleep.

'What an insensible blockhead that man is!' said Mr Sims, the middle-aged passenger; looking across the deck contemptuously at Mr Smallchild.

'If the sea had the same effect on you that it has on him,' retorted the invalid passenger, Mr Purling, 'you would be just as insensible yourself.'

Mr Purling (who was a man of sentiment) disagreed with Mr Sims (who was a man of business) on every conceivable subject, all through the voyage. Before, however, they could continue the dispute about Mr Smallchild, the doctor surprised them by appearing from the cabin.

'Any news from below, Jolly?' asked the captain, anxiously.

'None whatever,' answered the doctor. 'I've come to idle the afternoon away up here, along with the rest of you.'

As events turned out, Mr Jolly idled away an hour and a half exactly. At the end of that time, Mrs Drabble, the stewardess, appeared with a face of mystery, and whispered nervously to the doctor:

'Please to step below directly, sir.'

'Which of them is it?' asked Mr Jolly.

'*Both* of them,' answered Mrs Drabble, emphatically.

The doctor looked grave; the stewardess looked frightened. The two immediately disappeared together.

'I suppose, gentlemen,' said Captain Gillop, addressing Mr Purling, Mr Sims, and the first mate, who had just joined the party, 'I suppose it's only fit and proper, in the turn things have taken, to shake up Mr Smallchild? And I don't doubt but what we ought to have the other husband handy, as a sort of polite attention under the circumstances. Pass the word forward there, for Simon Heavysides. Mr Smallchild, sir! rouse up! Here's your good lady—— Hang me, gentlemen, if I know exactly how to put it to him.'

'Yes. Thank you,' said Mr Smallchild, opening his eyes drowsily. 'Biscuit and cold bacon, as usual – when I'm ready. I'm not ready yet. Thank you. Good afternoon.' Mr Smallchild closed his eyes again, and became, in the doctor's phrase, 'totally comatose.'

Before Captain Gillop could hit on any new plan for rousing this imperturbable passenger, Simon Heavysides once more approached the quarter-deck.

'I spoke a little sharp to you, just now, my man,' said the captain, 'being worried in my mind by what's going on on board this vessel. But I'll make it up to you, never fear. Here's your wife in, what they call, an interesting situation. It's only right you should be within easy hail of her. I look upon you, Heavysides, as a steerage-passenger in difficulties; and I freely give you leave to stop here along with us till it's all over.'

'You are very good, sir,' said Simon; 'and I am indeed thankful to you and to these gentlemen. But, please to remember, I have seven children already in the steerage – and there's nobody left to mind 'em but me. My wife has got over it uncommonly well, sir, on seven previous occasions – and I don't doubt but what she'll conduct herself in a similar manner on the eighth. It will be a satisfaction to her mind, Captain Gillop and gentlemen, if she knows I'm out of the way, and minding the children. For which reason, I respectfully take my leave.' With those words, Simon made his bow, and returned to his family.

'Well, gentlemen, these two husbands take it easy enough, at any rate!' said the captain. 'One of them is used to it, to be sure; and the other is——'

Here a banging of cabin doors below, and a hurrying of footsteps, startled the speaker and his audience into momentary silence and attention.

'Ease her with the helm, Williamson!' said Captain Gillop, addressing the man who was steering the vessel. 'In my opinion, gentlemen, the less the ship pitches the better, in the turn things are taking now.'

The afternoon wore on into evening, and evening into night.

Mr Smallchild performed the daily ceremonies of his nautical existence as punctually as usual. He was aroused to a sense of Mrs Smallchild's situation when he took his biscuit and bacon; lost the sense again when the time came round for 'squaring his accounts'; recovered it in the interval which ensued before he went to sleep: lost it again, as a matter of course, when his eyes closed once more – and so on through the evening and early night. Simon Heavysides received messages occasionally (through the captain's care), telling him to keep his mind easy; returned messages mentioning that his mind was easy, and that the children were pretty quiet, but never approached the deck in his own person. Mr Jolly now and then showed himself; said 'All right, – no news;' took a little light refreshment, and disappeared again, as cheerful as ever. The fair breeze still held; the captain's temper remained unruffled; the man at the helm eased the vessel, from time to time, with the most anxious consideration. Ten o'clock came: the moon rose and shone superbly; the nightly grog made its appearance on the quarter-deck; the captain gave the passengers the benefit of his company; and still nothing happened. Twenty minutes more of suspense slowly succeeded each other – and then, at last, Mr Jolly was seen suddenly to ascend the cabin stairs.

To the amazement of the little group on the quarter-deck, the doctor held Mrs Drabble, the stewardess, fast by the arm, and, without taking the slightest notice of the captain or the passengers, placed her on the nearest seat he could find. As he did this, his face became visible in the moonlight, and displayed to the startled spectators an expression of blank consternation.

'Compose yourself, Mrs Drabble,' said the doctor, in tones of unmistakable alarm. 'Keep quiet, and let the air blow over you. Collect yourself, ma'am – for Heaven's sake, collect yourself!'

Mrs Drabble made no answer. She beat her hands vacantly on her knees, and stared straight before her, like a woman panic-stricken.

'What's wrong?' asked the captain, setting down his glass of grog in dismay. 'Anything amiss with those two unfortunate women?'

'Nothing,' said the doctor. 'Both doing admirably well.'

'Anything queer with their babies?' continued the captain. 'Are there more than you bargained for, Jolly? Twins, for instance?'

'No! no!' replied Mr Jolly, impatiently. 'A baby apiece – both boys – both in first-rate condition. Judge for yourselves,' added the doctor, as the two new cabin-passengers tried their lungs, below, for the first time, and found that they answered their purpose in the most satisfactory manner.

'What the devil's amiss, then, with you and Mrs Drabble?' persisted the captain, beginning to lose his temper again.

'Mrs Drabble and I are two innocent people, and we have got into the most dreadful scrape that ever you heard of!' was Mr Jolly's startling answer.

The captain, followed by Mr Purling and Mr Sims, approached the doctor with looks of horror. Even the man at the wheel stretched himself over it as far as he could to hear what was coming next. The only uninterested person present was Mr Smallchild. His time had come round for going to sleep again, and he was snoring peacefully, with his biscuit and bacon close beside him.

'Let's hear the worst of it at once, Jolly,' said the captain, a little impatiently.

The doctor paid no heed to his request. His whole attention was absorbed by Mrs Drabble. 'Are you better now, ma'am?' he asked, anxiously.

'No better in my mind,' answered Mrs Drabble, beginning to beat her knees again. 'Worse, if anything.'

'Listen to me,' said Mr Jolly, coaxingly. 'I'll put the whole case over again to you, in a few plain questions. You'll find it all come back to your memory, if you only follow me attentively, and if you take time to think and collect yourself before you attempt to answer.'

Mrs Drabble bowed her head in speechless submission – and listened. Everybody else on the quarter-deck listened, except the impenetrable Mr Smallchild.

'Now, ma'am!' said the doctor. 'Our troubles began in Mrs Heavysides' cabin, which is situated on the starboard side of the ship?'

'They did, sir,' replied Mrs Drabble.

'Good! We went backwards and forwards, an infinite number of times, between Mrs Heavysides (starboard) and Mrs Smallchild (larboard) – but we found that Mrs Heavysides, having got the start, kept it – and when I called out, "Mrs Drabble! here's a chopping boy for you: come and take him!" – I called out starboard, didn't I?'

'Starboard, sir – I'll take my oath of it,' said Mrs Drabble.

'Good, again! "Here's a chopping boy," I said. "Take him, ma'am, and make him comfortable in the cradle." And you took him, and made him comfortable in the cradle, accordingly? Now, where was the cradle?'

'In the main cabin, sir,' replied Mrs Drabble.

'Just so! In the main cabin, because we hadn't got room for it in either of the sleeping cabins. You put the starboard baby (otherwise Heavysides) in the clothes-basket cradle in the main cabin. Good, once more. How was the cradle placed?'

'Crosswise to the ship, sir,' said Mrs Drabble.

'Crosswise to the ship? That is to say, with one side longwise towards the stern of the vessel, and one side longwise towards the bows. Bear that in mind – and now follow me a little farther. No! no! don't say you can't, and your head's in a whirl. My next question will steady it. Carry your mind on half an hour, Mrs Drabble. At the end of half an hour, you heard my voice again; and my voice called out – "Mrs Drabble! here's another chopping boy for you: come and take him!" – and you came and took him larboard, didn't you?'

'Larboard, sir, I don't deny it,' answered Mrs Drabble.

'Better and better! "Here is another chopping boy," I said. "Take him, ma'am, and make him comfortable in the cradle, along with number one." And you took the larboard baby (otherwise Smallchild), and made him comfortable in the cradle along with the starboard baby (otherwise Heavysides), accordingly? Now, what happened after that?'

'Don't ask me, sir!' exclaimed Mrs Drabble, losing her self-control, and wringing her hands desperately.

'Steady, ma'am! I'll put it to you as plain as print. Steady! and listen to me. Just as you had made the larboard baby comfortable, I had occasion to send you into the starboard (or Heavysides) cabin, to fetch something which I wanted in the larboard (or Smallchild) cabin; I kept you there a little while along with me; I left you, and went into the Heavysides cabin, and called to you to bring me something I wanted out of the Smallchild cabin, but before you got half-way across the main cabin, I said "No; stop where you are, and I'll come to you"; immediately after which, Mrs Smallchild alarmed you, and you came across to me of your own accord; and, thereupon, I stopped you in the main cabin, and said, "Mrs Drabble, your mind's getting confused, sit down and collect your scattered intellects"; and you sat down, and tried to collect them——?'

('And couldn't, sir,' interposed Mrs Drabble, parenthetically. 'Oh, my head! my head!')

— 'And tried to collect your scattered intellects, and couldn't?' continued the doctor. 'And the consequence was, when I came out from the Smallchild cabin to see how you were getting on, I found you with the clothes-basket cradle hoisted up on the cabin table, staring down at the babies inside with your mouth dropped open, and both your hands twisted in your hair? And when I said, "Anything wrong with either of those two fine boys, Mrs Drabble?" you caught me by the coat-collar, and whispered in my right ear these words: "Lord save us and help us, Mr Jolly, I've confused the two babies in my mind, and I don't know which is which!"'

'And I don't know now!' cried Mrs Drabble, hysterically. 'Oh, my head! my head! I don't know now!'

'Captain Gillop and gentlemen,' said Mr Jolly, wheeling round and addressing his audience with the composure of sheer despair, 'that is the Scrape – and, if you ever heard of a worse one, I'll trouble you to compose this miserable woman by mentioning it immediately.'

Captain Gillop looked at Mr Purling and Mr Sims. Mr Purling and Mr Sims looked at Captain Gillop. They were all three thunderstruck – and no wonder.

'Can't *you* throw any light on it, Jolly?' inquired the captain, who was the first to recover himself.

'If you knew what I have had to do below, you wouldn't ask me such a question as that,' replied the doctor. 'Remember that I have had the lives of two women and two children to answer for – remember that I have been cramped up in two small sleeping-cabins, with hardly room to turn round in, and just light enough from two miserable little lamps to see my hand before me – remember the professional difficulties of the situation, the ship rolling about under me all the while, and the stewardess to compose into the bargain; – bear all that in mind, will you, and then tell me how much spare time I had on my hands for comparing two boys together inch by inch – two boys born at night, within half an hour of each other, on board a ship at sea. Ha! ha! I only wonder the mothers and the boys and the doctor are all five of them alive to tell the story!'

'No marks on one or other of them, that happened to catch your eye?' asked Mr Sims.

'They must have been strongish marks to catch my eye in the light I had to work by, and in the professional difficulties I had to grapple with,' said the doctor. 'I saw they were both straight, well-formed children – and that's all I saw!'

'Are their infant features sufficiently developed to indicate a family likeness?' inquired Mr Purling. 'Should you say they took after their fathers or their mothers?'

'Both of them have light eyes, and light hair – such as it is,' replied Mr Jolly, doggedly. 'Judge for yourself.'

'Mr Smallchild has light eyes and light hair,' remarked Mr Sims.

'And Simon Heavysides has light eyes and light hair,' rejoined Mr Purling.

'I should recommend waking Mr Smallchild, and sending for Heavysides, and letting the two fathers toss up for it,' suggested Mr Sims.

'The parental feeling is not to be trifled with in that heartless manner,' retorted Mr Purling. 'I should recommend trying the Voice of Nature.'

'What may that be, sir?' inquired Captain Gillop, with great curiosity.

'The maternal instinct,' replied Mr Purling. 'The mother's intuitive knowledge of her own child.'

'Ay, ay!' said the captain. 'Well thought of. What do you say, Jolly, to the Voice of Nature?'

The doctor held up his hand impatiently. He was engaged in resuming the effort to rouse Mrs Drabble's memory by a system of amateur cross-examination, with the unsatisfactory result of confusing her more hopelessly than ever.

Could she put the cradle back, in her own mind, into its original position? No. Could she remember whether she laid the starboard baby (otherwise Heavysides) on the side of the cradle nearest the stern of the ship, or nearest the bows? No. Could she remember any better about the larboard baby (otherwise Smallchild)? No. Why did she move the cradle on to the cabin table, and so bewilder herself additionally, when she was puzzled already? Because it came over her, on a sudden, that she had forgotten, in the dreadful confusion of the time, which was which; and of course she wanted to look closer at them, and see; and she couldn't see; and to her dying day she should never forgive herself; and let them throw her overboard, for a miserable wretch, if they liked, – and so on, till the persevering doctor was wearied out at last, and gave up Mrs Drabble, and gave up, with her, the whole case.

'I see nothing for it but the Voice of Nature,' said the captain, holding fast to Mr Purling's idea. 'Try it, Jolly – you can but try it.'

'Something must be done,' said the doctor. 'I can't leave the women alone any longer; and the moment I get below they will both ask for their babies. Wait here, till you're fit to be seen, Mrs Drabble, and then follow me. Voice of Nature!' added Mr Jolly, contemptuously, as he descended the cabin stairs. 'Oh yes, I'll try it – much good the Voice of Nature will do us, gentlemen. You shall judge for yourselves.'

Favoured by the night, Mr Jolly cunningly turned down the dim lamps in the sleeping cabins to a mere glimmer, on the pretext that the light was bad for his patients' eyes. He then took up the first of the two unlucky babies that came to hand, marked the clothes in which it was wrapped with a blot of ink, and carried it in to Mrs Smallchild, choosing her cabin merely because he happened to be nearest to it. The second baby (distinguished by having no mark) was taken by Mrs Drabble to Mrs Heavysides. For a certain time, the two mothers and the two babies were left together. They were then separated again by medical order; and were afterwards reunited, with the difference that the marked baby went on this occasion to Mrs Heavysides, and the unmarked baby to Mrs Smallchild – the result, in the obscurity of the sleeping cabins, proving to be that one baby did just as well as the other, and that the Voice of Nature was (as Mr Jolly had predicted) totally incompetent to settle the existing difficulty.

'While night serves us, Captain Gillop, we shall do very well,' said the doctor, after he had duly reported the failure of Mr Purling's suggested experiment. 'But when morning comes, and daylight shows the difference between the children, we must be prepared with a course of some kind. If the two mothers, below, get the slightest suspicion of the case as it really stands, the nervous shock of the discovery may do dreadful mischief. They must be kept deceived, in the interests of their own health. We must choose a baby for each of them when to-morrow comes, and then hold to the choice, till the mothers are well and up again. The question is, who's to take the responsibility? I don't usually stick at trifles – but I candidly admit that *I'm* afraid of it.

'I decline meddling in the matter, on the ground that I am a perfect stranger,' said Mr Sims.

'And I object to interfere, from precisely similar motives,' added Mr Purling; agreeing for the first time with a proposition that emanated from his natural enemy all through the voyage.

'Wait a minute, gentlemen,' said Captain Gillop. 'I've got this difficult matter, as I think, in its right bearings. We must make a clean breast of it to the husbands, and let *them* take the responsibility.'

'I believe they won't accept it,' observed Mr Sims.

'And I believe they will,' asserted Mr Purling, relapsing into his old habits.

'If they won't,' said the captain, firmly, 'I'm master on board this ship — and, as sure as my name is Thomas Gillop, *I'll* take the responsibility!'

This courageous declaration settled all difficulties for the time being; and a council was held to decide on future proceedings. It was resolved to remain passive until the next morning, on the last faint chance that a few hours' sleep might compose Mrs Drabble's bewildered memory. The babies were to be moved into the main cabin before the daylight grew bright — or, in other words, before Mrs Smallchild or Mrs Heavysides could identify the infant who had passed the night with her. The doctor and the captain were to be assisted by Mr Purling, Mr Sims, and the first mate, in the capacity of witnesses: and the assembly so constituted was to meet, on consideration of the emergency of the case, at six o'clock in the morning, punctually.

At six o'clock, accordingly, with the weather fine, and the wind still fair, the proceedings began. For the last time Mr Jolly cross-examined Mrs Drabble, assisted by the captain, and supervised by the witnesses. Nothing whatever was elicited from the unfortunate stewardess. The doctor pronounced her confusion to be chronic, and the captain and the witnesses unanimously agreed with him.

The next experiment tried was the revelation of the true state of the case to the husbands.

Mr Smallchild happened, on this occasion, to be 'squaring his accounts' for the morning; and the first articulate words which escaped him in reply to the disclosure, were: 'Devilled biscuit and anchovy paste.' Further perseverance merely elicited an impatient request that they would 'pitch him overboard at once, and the two babies along with him.' Serious remonstrance was tried next, with no better effect. 'Settle it how you like,' said Mr Smallchild, faintly.' Do you leave it to me, sir, as commander of this vessel?' asked Captain Gillop. (No answer.) 'Nod your head, sir, if you can't speak.' Mr Smallchild nodded his head roundwise on his pillow – and fell asleep. 'Does that count for leave to me to act?' asked Captain Gillop of the witnesses. And the witnesses answered, decidedly, Yes.

The ceremony was then repeated with Simon Heavysides, who responded, as became so intelligent a man, with a proposal of his own for solving the difficulty.

'Captain Gillop and gentlemen,' said the carpenter, with fluent and melancholy politeness, 'I should wish to consider Mr Smallchild before myself in this matter. I am quite willing to part with my baby (whichever he is); and I respectfully propose that Mr Smallchild should take *both* the children, and so make quite sure that he has really got possession of his own son.'

The only immediate objection to this ingenious proposition was started by the doctor; who sarcastically inquired of Simon 'what he thought Mrs Heavysides would say to it?' The carpenter confessed that this consideration had escaped him; and that Mrs Heavysides was only too likely to be an irremovable obstacle in the way of the proposed arrangement. The witnesses all thought so too; and Heavysides and his idea were dismissed together, after Simon had first gratefully expressed his entire readiness to leave it all to the captain.

'Very well, gentlemen,' said Captain Gillop. 'As commander on board, I reckon next after the husbands in the matter of responsibility – I have considered this difficulty in all its bearings – and I'm prepared to deal with it. The Voice of Nature (which you proposed, Mr Purling) has been found to fail. The tossing up for it (which you proposed, Mr Sims) doesn't square altogether with my notions of what's right in a very serious business. No, sir! I've got my own plan; and I'm now about to try it. Follow me below, gentlemen, to the steward's pantry.'

The witnesses looked round on one another in the profoundest astonishment – and followed.

'Pickerel,' said the captain, addressing the steward, 'bring out the scales.'

The scales were of the ordinary kitchen sort, with a tin tray, on one side, to hold the commodity to be weighed, and a stout iron slab on the other, to support the weights. Pickerel placed these scales upon a neat little pantry table, fitted on the ball-and-socket principle, so as to save the breaking of crockery by swinging with the motion of the ship.

'Put a clean duster in the tray,' said the captain. 'Doctor,' he continued, when this had been done, 'shut the doors of the sleeping-berths (for fear of the women hearing anything); and oblige me by bringing those two babies in here.'

'Oh, sir!' exclaimed Mrs Drabble, who had been peeping guiltily into the pantry – 'oh, don't hurt the little dears! If anybody suffers, let it be me!'

'Hold your tongue, if you please, ma'am,' said the captain. 'And keep the secret of these proceedings, if you wish to keep your place. If the ladies ask for their children, say they will have them in ten minutes' time.'

The doctor came in, and set down the clothes-basket cradle on the pantry floor. Captain Gillop immediately put on his spectacles, and closely examined the two unconscious innocents who lay beneath him.

'Six of one, and half-a-dozen of the other,' said the captain. 'I don't see any difference between them. Wait a bit, though! Yes, I do. One's a bald baby. Very good. We'll begin with that one. Doctor, strip the bald baby, and put him in the scales.'

The bald baby protested – in his own language – but in vain. In two minutes he was flat on his back in the tin tray, with the clean duster under him to take the chill off.

'Weigh him accurately, Pickerel,' continued the captain. 'Weigh him, if necessary, to an eighth of an ounce. Gentlemen! watch this proceeding closely: it's a very important one.'

While the steward was weighing and the witnesses were watching, Captain Gillop asked his first mate for the log-book of the ship, and for pen and ink.

'How much, Pickerel?' asked the captain, opening the book.

'Seven pounds, one ounce, and a quarter,' answered the steward.

'Right, gentlemen?' pursued the captain.

'Quite right,' said the witnesses.

'Bald child – distinguished as Number One – weight, seven pounds, one ounce, and a quarter (avoirdupois),' repeated the captain, writing down the entry in the log-book. 'Very good. We'll put the bald baby back now, doctor; and try the hairy one next.'

The hairy one protested – also in his own language – and also in vain.

'How much, Pickerel?' asked the captain.

'Six pounds, fourteen ounces, and three-quarters,' replied the steward.

'Right, gentlemen?' inquired the captain.

'Quite right,' answered the witnesses.

'Hairy child – distinguished as Number Two – weight, six pounds, fourteen ounces, and three-quarters (avoirdupois),' repeated and wrote the captain. 'Much obliged to you, Jolly – that will do. When you have got the other baby back in the cradle, tell Mrs Drabble neither of them must be taken out of it, till further orders; and then be so good as to join me and these gentlemen on deck. If anything of a discussion rises up among us, we won't run the risk of being heard in the sleeping-berths.' With these words Captain Gillop led the way on deck, and the first mate followed with the log-book and the pen and ink.

'Now, gentlemen,' began the captain, when the doctor had joined the assembly, 'my first mate will open these proceedings by reading from the log a statement which I have written myself, respecting this business, from beginning to end. If you find it all equally correct with the statement of what the two children weigh, I'll trouble you to sign it, in your quality of witnesses, on the spot.'

The first mate read the narrative, and the witnesses signed it, as perfectly correct. Captain Gillop then cleared his throat, and addressed his expectant audience in these words:–

'You'll all agree with me, gentlemen, that justice is justice; and that like must to like. Here's my ship of five hundred tons, fitted with her spars accordingly. Say, she's a schooner of a hundred and fifty tons, the veriest landsman among you, in that case, wouldn't put such masts as these into her. Say, on the other hand, she's an Indiaman of a thousand tons, would our spars (excellent good sticks as they are, gentlemen) be suitable for a vessel of that capacity? Certainly not. A schooner's spars to a schooner, and a ship's spars to a ship, in fit and fair proportion.'

Here the captain paused, to let the opening of his speech sink well into the minds of the audience. The audience encouraged him with the parliamentary cry of 'Hear! hear!' The captain went on:—

'In the serious difficulty which now besets us, gentlemen, I take my stand on the principle which I have just stated to you. And my decision is as follows:— Let us give the heaviest of the two babies to the heaviest of the two women; and let the lightest then fall, as a matter of course, to the other. In a week's time, if this weather holds, we shall all (please God) be in port; and if there's a better way out of this mess than *my* way, the parsons and lawyers ashore may find it, and welcome.'

With those words the captain closed his oration; and the assembled council immediately sanctioned the proposal submitted to them, with all the unanimity of men who had no idea of their own to set up in opposition.

Mr Jolly was next requested (as the only available authority) to settle the question of weight between Mrs Smallchild and Mrs Heavysides, and decided it, without a moment's hesitation, in favour of the carpenter's wife, on the indisputable ground that she was the tallest and stoutest woman of the two. Thereupon, the bald baby, 'distinguished as Number One,' was taken into Mrs Heavysides' cabin; and the hairy baby, 'distinguished as Number Two,' was accorded to Mrs Smallchild; the Voice of Nature, neither in the one case nor in the other, raising the slightest objection to the captain's principle of distribution. Before seven o'clock, Mr Jolly reported that the mothers and sons, larboard and starboard, were as happy and comfortable as any four people on board ship could possibly wish to be; and the captain thereupon dismissed the council with these parting remarks:

'We'll get the studding-sails on the ship now, gentlemen, and make the best of our way to port. Breakfast, Pickerel, in half an hour, and plenty of it! I doubt if that unfortunate Mrs Drabble has heard the last of this business yet. We must all lend a hand, gentlemen, and pull her through if we can. In other respects, the job's over, so far as we are concerned; and the parsons and lawyers must settle it ashore.'

The parsons and the lawyers did nothing of the sort, for the plain reason that nothing was to be done. In ten days the ship was in port, and the news was broken to the two mothers. Each one of the two adored her baby, after ten days' experience of it – and each one of the two was in Mrs Drabble's condition of not knowing which was which.

Every test was tried. First, the test by the doctor, who only repeated what he had told the captain. Secondly, the test by personal resemblance; which failed in consequence of the light hair, blue eyes, and Roman noses, shared in common by the fathers, and the light hair, blue eyes, and no noses worth mentioning, shared in common by the children. Thirdly, the test of Mrs Drabble, which began and ended in fierce talking on one side, and floods of tears on the other. Fourthly, the test by legal decision, which broke down through the total absence of any instructions for the law to act on. Fifthly, and lastly, the test by appeal to the husbands, which fell to the ground in consequence of the husbands knowing nothing about the matter in hand. The captain's barbarous test by weight, remained the test still – and here am I, a man of the lower order, without a penny to bless myself with, in consequence.

Yes! I was the bald baby of that memorable period. My excess in weight settled my destiny in life. The fathers and mothers on either side kept the babies according to the captain's principle of distribution, in despair of knowing what else to do. Mr. Smallchild – who was sharp enough, when not sea-sick – made his fortune. Simon Heavysides persisted in increasing his family, and died in the workhouse.

Judge for yourself (as Mr Jolly might say) how the two boys born at sea have fared in after-life. I, the bald baby, have seen nothing of the hairy baby for years past. He may be short, like Mr Smallchild – but I happen to know that he is wonderfully like Heavysides, deceased, in the face. I may be tall like the carpenter – but I have the Smallchild eyes, hair, and expression, notwithstanding. Make what you can of that! You will find it come in the end to the same thing. Smallchild, junior, prospers in the world, because he weighed six pounds, fourteen ounces, and three-quarters. Heavyside, junior, fails in the world, because he weighed seven pounds, one ounce, and a quarter. Such is destiny, and such is life. I'll never forgive *my* destiny as long as I live. There is my grievance. I wish you good morning.